"I dare you..."

"No sex for one week."

"Sure," Levi said agreeably. "But if I take your dare, you take mine."

Ashley's hand shot up. "No. I'm done negotiating with you."

Of course he kept right on talking, as if she hadn't said anything. "For each night I go without sex, I get to choose a drink for you from Fantasy Island's cocktail menu."

She really, *really* needed to ignore the pulse of heat that suggestion generated in her stomach. And lower. This was *Levi*. She didn't even like him, but apparently her body thought angry sex was something she should try at least once in her life. Preferably tonight. He had her, and he knew it. She just couldn't walk away from a dare.

"You want to get me drunk?"

His teeth flashed as he snagged the drinks menu from the bar and waggled it in front of her. "We both know I'm talking about the other menu, babe. The secret menu, where the drink names are code for sexy stuff.

"I pick the drink. You do the deed..."

Dear Reader,

The idea for this book came to me while trolling Amazon looking for a fun, racy-but-not-so-racy-he-can't-open-it-in-public gift for my husband. Did you know you could buy dirty Truth or Dare games for couples? Let's just say I learned a thing or two. Levi Brandon and Ashley Dixon have plenty of learning to do about each other, as well. These two barely got along on their last undercover mission together, so discovering they might be accidentally married has sparks flying. Soon they're on Fantasy Island to sort out their marital status, but they can't stop fighting. Or daring each other. And the dares just get sexier and sexier...

Dares are a chance—a permission slip—to live out a secret fantasy. And what better time to do that when you're on a tropical island with a bad boy SEAL? Ashley is hardly a wild child (hello, she prefers to play by the rules), but rugged, sexy Levi tempts her to lose her inhibitions. And when she loses a bet and has to pay a very sensual forfeit, bringing her fantasies to life suddenly seems like the best of ideas.

Daring Her SEAL is the final story in my SEALs of Fantasy Island trilogy, which started with *Teasing Her SEAL* and then continued with *Pleasing Her SEAL*. Each couple has explored a very different set of sexy fantasies—and I hope you enjoy Levi and Ashley's story!

Happy reading,

Anne

Anne Marsh

Daring Her SEAL

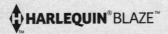

Recycling programs
for this product may
not exist in your area.

ISBN-13: 978-0-373-79895-7

Daring Her SEAL

Printed in U.S.A.

HARLEQUIN®
www.Harlequin.com

Anne Marsh writes sexy contemporary and paranormal romances because the world can always enjoy one more alpha male. She started writing romance after getting laid off from her job as a technical writer—and quickly decided happily-ever-afters trumped software manuals. She lives in Northern California with her family and six cats.

Books by Anne Marsh

Harlequin Blaze

Uniformly Hot!

Wicked Sexy
Wicked Nights
Wicked Secrets
Teasing Her SEAL
Pleasing Her SEAL

To get the inside scoop on Harlequin Blaze and its talented writers, be sure to check out BlazeAuthors.com.

All backlist available in ebook format.

Visit the Author Profile page at Harlequin.com for more titles.

For Lisa. Never, ever underestimate the power of your smile. I can't tell you too often that you're as fabulous as the heroine in any book and I'm rooting for your happily-ever-after.

1

"CAN YOU BE married without having sex?"

In all fairness, Levi Brandon needed the answer ASAP. His SEAL team leader paused, however, in the act of piling into the C-23 Sherpa transport aircraft as if Levi had farted in front of the President or something equally crass. The pained look on Gray Jackson's face was the only high point in Levi's day since he'd rolled out of bed for a dark o'clock training exercise only to discover that the US postal system and karma had caught up with him.

Gray slapped him on the back, harder than was strictly necessary. "Little personal, don't you think, Brandon?"

"I'm talking about myself, here," he said, humping his gear on board. The plane was a no-nonsense set of wings and wheels, perfect for the day's HALO training exercise.

While Gray mulled over his answer, the rest of SEAL Team Sigma loaded up with varying degrees of enthusiasm. Levi wasn't the only guy who felt jumping out of a plane at thirty thousand feet wasn't the best way to pass the time. He preferred keeping his feet on the ground or his fins in the water, thank you very much. On the other hand, at least when he jumped, he felt something. Even fear was marginally better than the emotional desert in which he usually existed.

"Last time I checked, you weren't married, planning on getting married, or even dating the same woman for consecutive nights. The better question is…can you go without having sex?" Gray dropped onto the bench beside Levi, buckling up as the door slammed shut and the plane started its taxi down the runway.

He'd tried dating when he was younger. Hell. The word *younger* made him feel like Methuselah, but the feeling wasn't inaccurate. Courtesy of Uncle Sam, he'd seen plenty and done more. The civilian women he'd dated once upon a time didn't understand what his job entailed. They'd seen the movies or read the books, but they still popped out perky *How was your day?*s like the words were Percocet. And too many times he'd been under orders not to discuss what had gone down.

Or he'd had days that were all training or sitting in a foxhole, waiting for the action to start. Nothing to talk about there, so he'd stayed mute and his gal of the moment had gotten upset. And then when shit did go down? What woman wanted to hear about the kill shot he made at long range or the building he'd cleared at the end of an M4? Sure as shooting, she hadn't been planning to help him pack for combat deployment, and he hadn't been packing socks and briefs, anyhow.

Sex was much simpler. He gave an orgasm; she got an orgasm. Or three. Everyone walked away happy, and the next time he jumped out of a plane there were no pesky emotional entanglements messing with his free fall.

He certainly had no plans for celibacy. On the other hand, fate had just slapped him with the moral equivalent of a chastity belt. Levi pulled the marriage certificate out of a pocket of his flight suit and waved it in the air. He needed a second opinion, and sure enough, Sam leaned over and snagged the paper. As the team medic, Sam Nale had even fewer personal boundaries than the rest of them, probably because he'd patched them all up on more than one occasion. Funny how once you'd had your fingers in a guy's bullet holes you felt like you knew him.

"Levi brought reading material." Sam unfolded the paper, read it over and whistled, the sound all but drowned out by the steady drone of the engines as the pilot took them to altitude. "And trouble. You're married?"

"Not on purpose," Levi admitted with a scowl.

Mason Black held out a hand for the certificate. "When did this happen?"

"I'm blaming you." Levi flipped Mason the bird. His teammate was a big bear of a SEAL, a damned good sniper, and the second member of their unit to find *true love* when they'd been undercover on Fantasy Island three months ago.

Not that Levi understood how two experienced warriors like Mason and Gray could fall in love while taking down a drug kingpin, but that was apparently what had happened. Levi had been looking forward to giving both of them crap about it for years to come—until he'd checked his mail this morning and discovered he had his own romantic woes to contend with.

"Your girl asked Ashley and I to be the stand-in bride and groom for a beach ceremony. She didn't tell us we were getting married for real."

Mason grinned. "Heads up. Every photo shoot with that woman is an adventure."

"Yeah," he grumbled, "but can you really imagine me married? To *Ashley*?"

Ashley Dixon had been a DEA tagalong on their last two missions. As far as he could tell she disliked everything about him—she'd been happy to detail her opinions loudly and at length. Naturally he'd given her plenty of shit while they'd been in their field together, and she'd *really* hated him calling her Mrs. Brandon after they'd played bride and groom for Mason's girl.

After they'd parted ways on Fantasy Island he hadn't thought of her once. Okay. He'd thought of her once. Maybe twice. She was gorgeous, they had a little history together and he wasn't dead yet although he was fairly certain he *would* be if he pursued her. She wasn't the kind of woman who shared her toys, and monogamy didn't work for him. So how the hell had he ended up married to her?

Mason returned the certificate and Levi jammed it back into his pocket. "Does Ashley know about this?"

He doubted it. "She hasn't said anything."

Because if she *had* known, she'd have found a way to tell him everything he'd done wrong that had led to an actual wedding—with an email, a phone call, or an RPG with a scathing note attached to the warhead. He'd butted heads with her every time he turned around on their past missions.

Well, every time except one. There *had* been that steamy alleyway kiss when they'd been surprised by a member of the motorcycle club they'd been investigating. He'd pinned Ashley against the wall and kissed her hard, because at the moment the only good excuse he could come up with for their presence in the alley was sex.

She'd kissed him back, too, in the interests of not jeopardizing their cover, but she'd made it clear later and in private that the next time his tongue got anywhere near her mouth she'd cut it off. His kiss had pissed her off *that* much, he thought with a smirk, and now he was gonna rile her up even more with his hey-babe-we're-married bomb. That was the only silver lining in this whole situation.

"Trickery's the only way Levi's getting our Ashley to say *yes*." Sam high-fived Mason. "Ten bucks says she'll skip the annulment and go straight to the *kill you* part of marriage. She gets to be a widow—you get to be dead. Problem solved."

Which was no fun at all. Levi would prefer to aggravate her, get underneath her defiant, snarky surface, if only because she was the one woman who'd never, ever contemplated saying *yes* to him.

Mason grinned. "I bet you can't get her to voluntarily say 'I do.'"

Levi wasn't Superman. No one could get Ashley to agree to anything she didn't want to do without wielding some powerful ammo. "Say 'I do' to what?"

"You." A big, obnoxious grin creased the face of the other SEAL.

"Are you doubting my powers of persuasion?"

The skeptical look Mason sported said that was an affirmative.

Gray cursed as if maybe, in some weird parallel universe, a Levi existed who actually *wanted* to be married to Ashley Dixon. "Ashley could out-stubborn a mule. She'd take a hell of a lot of persuading."

"Just a matter of leverage."

"Two minutes, ladies." Gray stood and motioned for the team to head to the back of the plane. Air tore through the cabin as the National Guardsmen chauffeuring them to the day's jump lowered the back ramp to reveal nothing but blue sky, empty air and a long drop to the landing zone. Levi slapped his hand on Sam's shoulder, taking up his position behind the other SEAL as he braced against the plane's upward pull.

He had never been wild about heights, but jumping out of a plane at thirty thousand feet beat the three-hour commute his brother bitched about, even if he was Navy and frogs weren't meant to fly. The good thing about HALO jumping, however, was that once he'd gotten his ass out the door, the hard part was done. Gravity took over, and as long he'd packed his chute correctly the happy ending was practically guaranteed.

"Ready?" Gray bellowed the words in Levi's ear, fighting to make himself heard over the slipstream's roar. "Don't make Ashley a widow. She's gonna want the chance to kill you herself."

"You betcha." He touched the knuckles of his free hand to Gray's. Seconds later, their team leader bellowed the order to jump and Sam flew out of the open bay. Gravity and the engine wake did their thing, sucking Levi out of the plane as he whooped, riding Sam's ass as they hung in the air for a long moment.

Then they plummeted through the air at terminal velocity, facedown, arms and feet up as strips of road and field swung in crazy circles beneath them. Seventy seconds of flying—or falling—and he pulled the rip cord at four thousand feet above ground level, popping his chute. On a mission rather than a training run, he might wait until as low as a thousand feet to minimize the amount of time hostiles had to spot him. Today, though, he'd maximize his chances of getting to the ground intact. If his chute failed, he'd still have time to deploy the back up. The chute shot out of his back, the canopy catching air and jerking him sharply upward. *Bingo.*

Sure, Ashley would prefer skipping the divorce and aiming straight for widowhood, but he had no intention of making it easy on her. If she wanted to get rid of him, she'd have to work for it.

2

His wife was fucking gorgeous.

Not that Levi deserved any kind of credit for Ashley's good looks, but if he had to end up accidentally married to a woman whose dislike for him made ISIS and the President of the United States seem like cozy besties, at least he'd scored a hot bride.

The assessment officially made him shallow, but he still couldn't wrap his head around the fact that they were legally married. The woman bent over her desk, working a cable behind the computer monitor while she sweet-talked the hardware, would rip him a new one when he shared the news with her. In the meantime, however, he might as well enjoy the show.

Husky phrases drifted to him. *Come on, baby. Work with me.* Yeah, he might get something out of this little field trip. Taunting Ashley was a helluva lot of fun.

He leaned against the doorframe. "You got computer woes too?"

The DEA's office sure wasn't Sexyville. After he'd breached the security at the front desk, he'd followed directions and ridden a beige elevator, taken two equally beige corridors, and then forded a sea of chest-high gray cubicles occupied by suits of both the male and female variety. Heads turned as he passed, because his off-duty jeans, motorcycle boots and black leather jacket weren't standard office wear. He hadn't come here to give a fashion show, though, so he kept moving.

After infiltrating third-world countries, locating Ashley's office was easy. Plus, the scenery was motivational. The way her skirt hugged the curves of her ass fed his Victoria's Secret fantasy, and her blouse wasn't half bad, either. The silky material draped over her boobs and he'd bet the fabric was as soft as the skin it only partially concealed. When she delved further into the tangle of cables, she flashed him the shadow of a black bra strap. *Hooyah.*

"Dixon?" he prompted, when she didn't look up from the mess of cables she was untangling.

She glanced his way automatically, a polite smile pasted to her face. Naturally her smile disappeared real quick when she realized who'd knocked on her door.

"You." Her voice held a wealth of disapproval, but that was nothing new. Frankly, he had a hard time imagining welcome, pleasure or anything remotely happy painted on her puss. She didn't like him, and he never seemed to get things right as far as she was concerned. Too bad, so sad. Wait until she heard what he had to say.

"In the flesh." He stepped into her office because he didn't need to attract any more attention from her floor mates. She had ten feet by ten feet to herself, along with three pieces of battered office furniture, a dusty plastic plant and a series of action figures suspended from the ceiling by what looked like fishing line. Stepping closer and blocking her access to the room's only exit, he offered her a lazy grin. "I didn't recognize you wearing clothes."

She'd rocked a very nice string bikini on their undercover mission to Fantasy Island, and…what? He was supposed to pretend he hadn't noticed? Hello. Parts of him were biologically incapable of *not* noticing, no matter how much vitriol she shot his way.

And bingo…her polite *can-I-help-you?* expression morphed into one hundred percent pissed-off female as she straightened up.

"I'm licensed to carry concealed. Don't make me shoot you."

Concealing a weapon in her current getup seemed challenging, but Ashley liked her guns and he'd seen her produce firearms from beneath the smallest of bandage dresses out in the field. He had no idea how she did it, but he respected the hell out of it. He also needed her to listen to him for five minutes.

She made a sound delightfully close to a snarl. How nice to know he still could get under her skin. Smiling at her, he said, "I need to talk to you. Take a smoke break."

Brown eyes narrowed. "It's *with* and not *to*. And smoking kills."

She put the desk between them. And while he enjoyed the way her ass wiggled in the skirt as she sauntered to her chair in three-inch heels, he still needed to talk to her. *With* her. She never missed an opportunity to point out that he was wrong, did she?

Of course, he also didn't care much about getting it right, so he advanced on her, flattening his palms on her desk. Naturally, the surface was all neat and tidy, her office supplies arranged at right angles and the folders stacked precisely. She'd never liked messes. When he deliberately nudged a pencil out of its careful row, she glared.

"We can do this the hard way. I can carry you out over my shoulder." His dick twitched at that. Hell. This was *Dixon*.

She didn't sit down, just folded her arms over her chest and inhaled as though she was trying to find her patience or her balance or something. "Step inside and shut the door."

Huh. Who knew he'd find *that* order a turn-on? It was likely only because he hadn't gotten laid in over a month. Lurking in foxholes wreaked havoc on a man's social life, and he'd come straight to Quantico once he'd arrived stateside. Ashley might be annoying as hell, but she deserved to know about their marriage, just in case she had any wedding plans of her own. He was in outright Boy Scout territory, making sure she didn't commit bigamy or mess up her taxes any. Maybe she'd even polish his halo for him. With her tongue.

Or she just might kill him. He'd give it even odds at the moment. She leaned toward him, not intimidated in the slightest.

She'd slicked her dark, glossy hair back from her face in a severe style that made her look all cheekbones. With less than two feet between them, he could smell her perfume, which was another first for him. She didn't wear that stuff in the field, and apparently he'd been missing out. She smelled like warmth and fruit and some kind of flower thing. Damned if he knew what it was, but he liked it. He should get a bottle and spray the boys in the foxhole next time he had to camp out for a week in the jungle.

She made a give-it-up gesture. "Some time this century, Brandon."

Given their eager audience—he'd counted ten agents and four secretaries plus a maintenance guy messing with a thermostat—he kicked the door shut with his booted foot. Probably not what she'd intended, but she should know by now that she needed to be specific with him.

"How do you want me?" he drawled, keeping his eyes on her. Her lips tightened. She was wearing lipstick in a nice nude shade. No flashy come-do-me red for her in the office. Did the agents she worked with know the calm ice-princess facade was a front? She had a wild child hiding underneath that gorgeous face, and she was a demon in the field. She would have made an excellent SEAL.

"Sit," she snapped, as if he was some kind of trained poodle. News flash. He only pretended to be civilized. If she didn't play nice, he didn't have to, either. He definitely wasn't planting his ass in a chair while she stood over him in the power position.

Time to take charge.

"If I sit like a good boy, will you park that pretty ass of yours on my lap?"

ASHLEY'S BRAIN SPLUTTERED to an outraged halt, because who *said* sexist stuff like that these days? Naturally, Levi used her momentary distraction to circle the desk between them. She hesitated a moment too long, distracted by the sexy SEAL prowling toward her. Dark hair buzzed short with military precision, brown eyes that crinkled at the corner when he laughed, and just the hint of a dimple in his right cheek…damn it. She'd seen him in action and the man was quick. He also fought dirty, and any words that came out of his mouth were just one more weapon. She should have remembered that.

He pulled her toward him until her thighs were plastered against him, his muscular, denim-covered leg thrusting between hers as he danced her backward smoothly. Her back hit the wall, her heart simultaneously taking a nosedive toward her stomach. Darn it. Being close to Levi was too much like riding a roller coaster.

A sexy, *dangerous* roller coaster with bad manners.

His big body radiated heat and carefully leashed power as he boxed her in, and she didn't know if she should take a moment to admire the sheer masculine ballsiness of the move—or knee him in the nuts on principle. She hadn't known he was in town, although it wasn't as though they shared social plans. They'd worked in the field together. Sometimes they'd killed together. None of which was drop-in-and-have-a-beer material.

His mouth shifted, brushing her ear. "Hello again, Mrs. Brandon."

How much trouble would she get in if she pulled her gun in the office? Because the thought of plugging Levi's fine ass with a bullet got more and more appealing by the moment.

"That joke got old about the twentieth time you trotted it out on Fantasy Island after we did the beach thing. Do I look like a *missus*? Maybe I missed the part where you tattooed *property of* on my ass."

She bent her knees, ducked under his arm and pushed him hard against the wall. He let her slam him into the paint job and that pissed her off even more. Life was one big joke to Levi Brandon and she hated it when he played with her.

"It's not a joke, babe. We're married."

"Uh-huh. Tell that one to the judge and back the hell off." That was another thing about Levi—he could deliver a joke with a perfectly straight face.

"You need to listen to me on this one." He flipped her around smoothly, face to the wall, wrists pinned over her head. Since the man had to have almost a hundred pounds on her, she was at a definite disadvantage in close quarters.

"Scared?" Sure, it wasn't nice to taunt him, but around him her inner five-year-old came out to play.

"Not exactly," he said cheerfully. "But someone's going to end up in the ER if we keep showing each other our moves. Plus kink's not my thing. I didn't come here to hurt you."

"So you're manhandling me to be *nice*?" She didn't bother hiding the disbelief in her voice. Truth was, Levi did what he wanted and he didn't worry about the consequences. It must be nice. She was also fairly certain he had a much broader acquaintance with *kink* than she did.

In answer, he kicked her legs wider, which was a challenge given the lack of give in her skirt. Heat hit her hard between her thighs, her panties dampening as she felt him against her back. *Chemical reaction.* That was all. Sure, it sucked that she got horny around Levi, but he came in a pretty package and looking at him had never been a hardship. It was when she had to listen to him that things went to hell.

It took him less than fifteen seconds to find the gun

tucked in the small of her back. He slipped it out of her waistband and set it on her desk. "Sexy."

"Back off and tell me why you're here." Had the Marcos brothers managed to shake the charges against them? If they'd been assigned a third mission together, surely the special agent in charge would have notified her.

"You think I need a reason to be here? Maybe I had a couple of weeks of leave coming to me and just missed your lovely face." He pressed harder against her, tucking his dick against her butt as if he had some kind of right to do so. Clearly, it had been too long since she'd had sex—working undercover with SEAL teams had definitely put a crimp in her social life—because she couldn't even work up much outrage at his erection. He was huge, he was turned on and apparently her sexual drought had lasted long enough that she was willing to cut him some slack. *Sucker* her brain crowed at her libido.

"Well, I'm not helping you with *that*." She wriggled her butt against his front just to make her point and he hissed.

"Yeah. Don't worry about it. Dick's got a mind of its own and it really, really likes your skirt."

And that was the problem with Levi. The outside package was hot—*hello*, she'd never met an ugly SEAL—but then he opened his mouth. Too bad she couldn't duct tape his lips shut and just admire the view.

"Could you be more offensive? Is this your idea of a joke?" Because she didn't feel like laughing and she was this close to kneeing him in the balls the next chance she got.

"You hear a punch line coming out of my mouth?"

"You want to know how many practical jokes I've been the butt of over the years? When you're the only female on a team, you hear it all."

He whistled. "You work with some nasty people, Dixon."

She drove her head back, pulling free of his hold and swinging her elbow toward his cheekbone. If she accidentally introduced his head to her desk on his way down, she didn't care. He hit the floor with a thud and a laugh, twisting to avoid her office furniture. Great. The agents on the floor below would be banging on the ceiling.

Grabbing her gun, she loaded it with swift efficiency while he rolled lightly to his feet. "A vagina doesn't make me stupid."

He gave her a look she couldn't interpret. "I've never thought you were stupid."

Well. Okay, then.

He grinned at her and kept right on running his mouth. Levi never had known when to quit. "Deadly. Irritating as hell. Adorably geeky when you get your computer on. Those adjectives all work for me, although after you seeing you in your skirt, I'm adding sexy because I believe in calling it like I see it. You should dress up for me more often, babe." Chuckling with amusement, he added, "I have nothing but respect for your skills. I just give you shit because I give all my guys crap."

She pretended she didn't feel a small spurt of warmth at his compliment. After all, she was still debating hurting him.

"I'm just one of the guys now? Go away." She dropped into her office chair and motioned toward her door with the gun. She'd left the safety on, which was more than he deserved. "That was fun. We've got to stop meeting like this."

He leaned against the edge of her desk and fished an envelope out of his jacket. "We're married. Read for yourself."

She opened it and pulled out a fancy-schmancy certificate with black calligraphy and plenty of gold foil. Once upon a time, the thing had probably been elegant as hell, but now it was full of creases from repeated folding. Hot sauce decorated one corner. Obviously, whatever it was, he highly valued it. *Not.*

The letter was addressed to Mr. and Mrs. Brandon and she got a bad, bad feeling in her stomach. "This is dated three weeks ago."

He shrugged. "I was in a foxhole. The postal service doesn't deliver out there."

She read on and froze. "How can we possibly be married?"

"I imagine it was that part where the minister asked us if we 'did.' Shoulda lied, babe."

"That was a fake ceremony." She set the papers on her desk. Levi had to be joking for some sick, twisted, unfathomable reason. They couldn't be *married.* They were the two least compatible people on the planet, not to mention she'd sworn off marriage after watching her parents' union explode so spectacularly.

And if those weren't good enough reasons, she had a performance review in four weeks, and a congressional hearing to attend in two. She'd blown the whistle on a team of DEA agents who'd treated their Central American posting as party central under the mistaken assumption that they could do whatever they wanted with impunity, so it definitely wouldn't look good if it came out that she'd been involved in a fake wedding ceremony in Belize. A ceremony where the *real* bride and groom were supposed to be a notorious drug kingpin and his girlfriend, but they'd been a no-show because they'd been arrested and carted out to international waters by an undercover SEAL team. She could practically see the headlines now: DEA Agent Is Wedding Proxy for Drug Lord.

Levi lifted his broad shoulders in another shrug. "Apparently, the minister didn't get the memo and someone in the registry department agrees with him—and sent us that commemorative piece of paper."

"It has to be a prank." God knew, the SEALs loved a good joke. This one seemed kind of elaborate, but sometimes the guys had too much thinking time on their hands. "Did you call the registry department and verify this? Or do you believe anything someone writes on a piece of paper?"

"The registry department," Levi said tightly, "apparently had a close encounter with a tropical rainstorm two weeks ago. Most of the roof went and the filing system took a direct hit. No one is answering the phones because half the staff is on leave while the government rebuilds. The half of the staff that is still working has neither the time nor the inclination to wade through thousands of waterlogged pieces of paper looking for a certificate that might or might not be there."

Ouch.

"Since it's easy to blow someone off when there's two thousand miles between you and them, I planned on going down there since I had some leave coming to me," Levi continued. "Because I assumed you'd want this taken care of."

For once, she had to agree with him. "If this is true, I want a divorce."

Immediately. How fast could you get divorced in Belize?

"I wasn't looking for a life sentence, either."

No. It had to be a fake, a joke, anything other than real. "We can't possibly be married. Whatever you did, fix it." She slapped the papers against his chest.

"How is this *my* fault?" He got that stubborn, badass look on his face, but to hell with him. He didn't scare her and she was tired of his crap.

"You're here. You're the one telling me we're married. Prove it to me."

He yanked the hem of his T-shirt up, revealing flat abs and, God, a perfect six-pack. "You want to skip straight to the honeymoon? Good idea."

"You pig. Do not get naked in my office." Ashley pokered up the second he flashed her.

Ice queen didn't like his approach? Too damn bad.

She didn't get to tell him what to do. This mess wasn't his fault. Of course, if he was being honest, it wasn't hers either, but he didn't feel like being fair right now. Hell, he'd just discovered that he was married to a woman who wanted to murder him. It hadn't been a good week.

He leaned in and delivered his ultimatum. "Put in for vacation time, because we need to go down there and sort it out."

If looks could kill, he'd be dead, planted and decaying. Vacationing with him was apparently *not* on her bucket list, but she'd just have to get over it. If he had to deal with this, so did she.

"It can't be legal. We didn't fill out an application or sign anything. This isn't my fault."

And that automatically made it his?

"You can't make me go," she continued petulantly. Fighting words. Yeah…she was pissed off, all right. He entertained the idea of unloading her gun, but he wasn't suicidal.

"I think I can." He knew the look she got when she was thinking about taking him out, and chances were his teammates had been right. Given the right opportunity, she'd skip the annulment and go straight for the kill shot.

"Really?" She drawled the question and his blood pressure soared. "Walk me through it, big guy."

Jesus. Maybe, just once, she could lay off the sarcasm and admit that he was right. It wasn't even like he *wanted* to be right about their just-married status. He'd have been deliriously happy to find out he'd been mistaken. "I'm not the one who has something to lose."

She smiled and, okay, it was probably wrong that the mean look she got right before she went after him turned him on so much. He had a kink in his think that he should work on. Later. After he was single again. "Did you ask permission of your commanding officer before you went and got yourself married on a mission?"

"Nope, but I'm thinking the worst I get is an ass-chewing for being dumb enough to stand in for the groom." His unit had already made it clear they'd never let him live the marriage down. They'd started calling him Wedding Ken and one wiseass had bought him a pair of matching his-and-hers ring pops. "But I can go out and announce to all of your colleagues that we're married."

She didn't back down. "Awkward, but I'll live."

One of the useful things about Ashley was that she froze when she lied. She probably didn't realize that she stilled, as if all of the brain cells in that downright enormous brain of hers diverted to creative thinking and forgot to keep her body in motion. The way she'd stopped moving when she'd dismissed his threat screamed concern. All he needed to do was push a wee bit harder and she'd be on that plane with him.

"I'll give them all the details, Dixon. With *photos*. You in a white bikini with *BRIDE* bedazzled over your perky little ass."

"You wore matching swim trunks," she pointed out, her magnificent boobs rising and falling as her temper picked up steam. The top button on her blouse was in serious danger of blowing, a development that he'd enjoy as he had nothing but admiration for her breasts, but she'd care. Maybe he'd let her know. In a minute. Or six.

"I passed your HR department on the way in." He grinned, keeping half an eye on that button. "Shall I plan on making a pit stop there...?"

"What are they going to do? Throw me a bridal shower?" The button didn't budge, damn it, but a mocking smile curved her lips. Kissing the smirk away became his new plan B.

"After I pay a visit to Human Resources, you'll be drowning in paperwork. I'll be on your life insurance, your 401K beneficiary form, and your DNR. You'll spend *years* untangling our lives. Plus, it's not like we eloped to Vegas on our downtime. We got hitched on a tropical island that promotes kinky sex."

She treated him to another eye roll. "I'm trying not to remember that part."

Then she was going to love what he had to say next.

"I read the news this morning. The DEA is in the middle of a sex scandal, babe, and some of your agents in a South American country that shall not be named? They liked to attend cartel-sponsored sex parties and Fantasy Island won't look good in that light. When you take the stand in the Marcos case in two weeks, the defense lawyer will have a field day with you."

He watched her gorgeous face as she chewed his words over. If Marcos's lawyer found out she and Levi had gotten married on a tropical island known for sex games, the headlines wouldn't be good. At best, her reputation would be shot. At worst, she'd be looking at a demotion or getting fired.

"You'd get in trouble too," she countered. Right. They'd covered his lack of permission from a superior officer—and his lack of concern. His wasn't a career-ending move even if Command wouldn't be thrilled. He hadn't been on leave and he sure hadn't asked permission—but he also hadn't thought he was really tying the knot.

"And I'll get a slap on the wrist. You want to risk your next promotion? Because I heard you had a once-in-a-lifetime opportunity that you're over the moon about."

"This is blackmail."

He shrugged. Having had some experience with skirting the grayer edges of the law, he knew better than to admit anything out loud.

"You're willing to commit a felony to force me to

accompany you?" Her voice rose, and the button on her blouse slipped further.

In answer, he blew her a kiss.

"You suck," she bit out.

"One hundred percent, babe." He definitely had her now. "I get the pleasure of your company for one week on Fantasy Island. You get radio silence about why we're headed out there and a bonus vacation at a swank resort."

"Two things." She held up a finger. "One, I always get even."

"Looking forward to it."

"Two, blow my credibility with my team, and I *will* kill you."

"Hey, you want me to go away." Christ, she'd felt good pinned beneath him. Marriage didn't have to be all bad. "Well, in order for that to happen, you got to give me something, starting with a divorce. You're coming with me, babe," he said, because he loved needling her and damned if this wasn't the first time in a long time he'd come out the clear winner in their battle of wits. Fighting with Dixon was tricky business.

She slammed her head against the back of her chair, fingers digging into the armrest. "Fuck."

He winked at her. "Only if you ask nicely."

3

FANTASY ISLAND LOOKED GOOD. Or maybe that was Ashley's unwilling company.

Ashley had pointedly ignored him on their flight from Virginia to Belize. They'd hitched a ride on a military carrier, so it hadn't been the kind of flight with peanuts and mile-high sex, which was too bad. She looked even better than the island, although he wasn't stupid enough to say that out loud with any degree of sincerity. She still wanted his head on a platter for the we're-married-for-real revelation he'd laid on her in Quantico. And, yeah, she was also sore about his making her come down to Belize. Too bad for her, because he liked pushing her buttons. She was cute as hell when she got mad.

She'd braided her hair back in a no-nonsense twist. The severe do, combined with her white T-shirt and khaki flight suit, shouldn't have been sexy. Unfortunately for him, he appeared to find everything about her attractive. She was like fire and he couldn't *not* touch.

He couldn't remember the last time he'd felt this kind of curiosity about anything, but he felt it in spades around Ashley and never mind that dragging her out here topped the list of stupid things he'd done in his lifetime. Sure, he probably could have handled all this himself via a couple of quick phone calls—even if the registry department was waterlogged and *sans* roof— but what fun would have *that* been? So, instead, he'd blackmailed her onto the military transport and then called in a few favors for a helicopter to make the hop from Belize City to Fantasy Island. He must have left his brain in his last foxhole or stood too close to a mortar round. That was the only explanation.

As soon as the bird hit the landing pad and the rotors stopped, Ashley was out and striding down the path. She hadn't even bothered grabbing her bag. He knew she didn't want to be here, but he hadn't realized she'd literally be running to check out their marriage ceremony. She was breaking all known speed records for tracking down a divorce and he didn't think it was because she only had a week's vacation time to spend on the island.

"You left your stuff," he hollered after her, ignoring the resort staff already moving in to grab their duffels. Problem solved, although he usually preferred to handle his own gear, and not just because he usually packed ammo instead of swim trunks.

She tossed him a saucy look over her shoulder. "Make yourself useful, Brandon."

"You want me to be your porter?" Like that was happening.

Screw it. He grabbed his own bag and hoofed it after her. He'd keep his stuff where he could see it, especially since he had a Glock and a few other toys cozied up with his skivvies. Fantasy Island should be safe as Fort Knox, but he hadn't survived this long by taking chances. He owed Ashley that much, at least. The helicopter started back up. Guess their pilot wasn't planning on sticking around.

She was already halfway down the path, speed walking as if she was competing for gold. Or maybe she just wanted to beat him to the front desk. Didn't matter. She could win all the minor skirmishes she wanted, but he'd won their war. She was here. He fell in beside her.

"You're a bad penny," she announced, not taking her gaze off the path in front of her. It was getting close to sunset, and the sunlight was filtering through the palm trees. Monkeys chattered away overhead, and the birds yelled back. Kind of like him and Dixon really. Plenty of noise but no real conversation.

He shot her a grin. "I do keep turning up, don't I?"

"What?" She gave him a hard look and he figured she was seconds away from elbowing him.

"Just thinking aloud," he said, because that was the truth. "So you think they got the bloodstains out of the gravel yet?"

They both looked at the road where they'd taken down Marcos. Everything seemed normal.

Ashley didn't stop her mad dash for freedom. "You'd better hope *they* don't remember your pretty face or connect it with the disappearance of the Marcos bridal party."

He honestly didn't expect it to be an issue. The staff had been rotated out since their last covert visit and people tended to see what they wanted to see anyhow.

When they made it to reception, naturally Ashley wasn't done fighting him. Since he'd booked the reservation, he ponied up his credit card—and she promptly whipped out hers. While they argued over who got the privilege of paying the bill, the stuffy guy at the front desk shoved wet towels and champagne drinks with ridiculous red cherries in their direction, as if cotton and alcohol could fix their relationship problems.

Not a chance in hell.

And honestly? It kind of bothered him that Ashley wouldn't let him take care of her. Fantasy Island's room rates were sky-high, and he didn't know if she had that kind of cash. He'd planned on blackmailing her—not bleeding her dry.

"You embarrassed the check-in guy," he pointed out when they were finally being whisked away to their villa in a golf cart. Stuffy Guy had eventually stepped in and solved the argument by taking *both* their credit cards.

She gave him the look he'd decided to christen Code Yellow. If it worked for Homeland Security, it worked for him. She wasn't ready to shove him out of the moving vehicle (Code Orange) or shoot him with his own weapon (Code Red), but neither was she volunteering to strip naked and fulfill all his sexual fantasies (Code Green). "We're going to have one of those modern marriages, where everybody pulls his or her own weight. Got it?"

Somehow, he didn't think that was really a question. "I made you come down here. I pay."

"It's not that simple, Brandon."

"Maybe you should call me Mr. Brandon. We could take the nineteenth century approach to our marital union." He kind of liked the sound of that but she huffed in response and drilled holes into the back of their driver's head.

"Actually, I'm gonna call you Blackmailing Bastard,"

she announced. The driver clearly didn't care for their hostilities, because the golf cart hurtled along the path as though it was shooting for liftoff. Guess the guy wanted to dump them ASAP and Levi could hardly blame him.

When they reached the villa, Ashley bounded ahead while Levi grabbed the bags and discreetly tipped their driver. He had no idea how come his charming bride hadn't cut *that* sexist gesture off at the pass, but he'd take it. As soon as he stepped inside, he spotted the enormous gift basket parked in the middle of a rose-covered bed. A single, really large bed.

Damn it. He hadn't had the best of connections when he'd called the resort to book a last-minute room. Apparently, the words *married* and *recently* had gotten mistranslated along the way into *I want hot sex in the honeymoon suite.*

Ordinarily, he'd have been fine with the misunderstanding—he had no problem with a little opportunistic sex—but this was Dixon. Having actual intercourse with her was as likely as peace in the Middle East or the zombie apocalypse. They'd have to compromise, however, and hopefully she wasn't a bed hog, because given what this place was costing him, he was *not* sleeping on the daybed, the floor or anyplace else that didn't offer a million-dollar mattress.

"Someone thinks we're on our honeymoon." She poked the basket and he had no idea how to interpret the strange look on her face. Ashley being Ashley, though, he figured she'd tell him exactly what she was thinking and then follow it up with multistep directions on how to do exactly what she wanted.

"Technically not wrong," he pointed out. "What did we score?"

She smiled. Slowly. Yeah, he might be newly married but he already knew he was in trouble here—and that was before she started pulling stuff out of the gift basket as if she was unloading cans of Campbell's from a grocery bag.

"We've got edible panties. Edible boxers." She arched an eyebrow. "Which probably offers more calories than your average woman consumes in a day, so you'll excuse me if I'm not feeling hungry."

She might not be, but he suddenly was. He dropped down onto the bed, shoving rose petals out of the way. "Are you playing show and tell?"

"You first." She snorted. "Some of this stuff should come with directions or an operating manual."

"Novice." He flicked her knee with his fingers.

"Because you're an expert with—" she squinted "—chocolate body butter?"

Not yet, but he could be. Licking the stuff off Ashley's body suddenly didn't seem half bad.

"We also have a pair of his and hers nipple clamps." She waved something around that looked like a medieval torture device in miniature. Or an eyelash curler. Apparently he *hadn't* seen everything in his bachelor days. "You could be a gentleman and volunteer to go first."

"Not a chance in hell." Not that he didn't like the mental image of him touching her nipples, but pain wasn't his thing. "Your boobs are too pretty to mark up."

She made a face he'd seen a dozen times in the field. He razzed her and she gave it right back. "Flatterer. You just like me for my boobs."

"And I'd like to keep mine in one piece," he said, grimacing slightly. Contrary to what she seemed to believe, he actually did have limits. Plus he truly did like more about her than her lovely anatomy. She was a damned good agent. He respected the way she single-mindedly went after her targets and showed no mercy. She knew her way around a gun. And she didn't hesitate to get dirty. Really dirty. There were four good reasons right there to like Ashley.

"And here we have our piéce de résistance—" She pulled an enormous purple dildo out of the bottom of the basket. "Apparently the resort staff isn't sure there's enough of you to keep me happy and have thoughtfully provided us with Purple Monster. Catch."

Karma was a bitch. Levi caught the dildo automatically, then looked at what he had in his hand. Yep. Twelve inches of battery-operated love machine. He opened his mouth. Closed it. Examined the toy again. It definitely merited a second glance because he was pretty sure fitting that much latex in anyone was an anatomical impossibility. Still, his brain did its best to imagine all sorts of scenarios involving Ashley, twelve inches of purple penis and himself.

"Enjoy," she said wryly. "I'm going to get a drink at the bar."

PLENTY OF ADJECTIVES described Levi. Infuriating came to mind. Along with stubborn, pain in her ass, aggravating, and…sexy. Her SEAL was hot. When he flashed her that devilish grin, she was torn between hitting him—and kissing him. Which was going to be her little secret. The look on his face when she'd tossed him that dildo had been pretty priceless. Too bad her phone had

been across the room, because a picture of him holding the purple monster would have been ideal coun-
ter-blackmail material—which she needed desperately
because he was a sneaky, conniving, underhanded bastard. He hadn't given her a choice about coming here,
and that pissed her off. She wasn't his beck-and-call
girl—or his wife, no matter what a piece of paper might
say—and the faster he understood that, the better.

Fortunately, the bar was right where she'd left it on
her last visit to Fantasy Island. Although her flight suit
and boots weren't resort wear, she needed to get out of
the villa.

Maybe she should head back to the front desk and
see if she could score a second room, because putting
some space between her and her irritatingly hot SEAL
seemed prudent. Plus if he was going to insist on paying for their stay here, she had a golden opportunity
for some good, old-fashioned revenge. She'd run up so
many room charges that his credit card would demand
a cease-fire. She could host an open bar and clean out
the gift shop—if there was anything left to buy after
all the welcome gifts that had been stockpiled for them
in the room.

God. She couldn't hold back a laugh as she recalled
his expression when she'd unpacked the basket. She'd
half suspected that he'd ordered the stuff just to get a
rise out of her, but the purple dildo had surprised him.

Not that she was usually into toys—and the twelve
inches of that particular device were just *too* optimis-
tic—but she could have been convinced. *No.* Bad libido. No convincing, no weakening, and *no* flirting
with the enemy.

She'd gotten her boots off, her pants rolled up and her

feet in the sand when Levi showed up a half hour later. Frankly, she was surprised he'd taken as long as he had. The man enjoyed torturing her and he definitely enjoyed a beer, so her presence at the resort's tiki bar was win-win for him. He was hard to miss where he stood in the bar's entrance, scanning the place for her. Six feet of hard, brawny SEAL made quite the impression.

And the way he sauntered across the bar toward her made her want to fan herself. The man was hot. He practically prowled, his movements powerful and self-assured as he came toward her. When he dropped onto the swing seat next to hers, the close-up was even better and since he hadn't opened his mouth yet? She could still enjoy the view. Almost immediately, he started whistling obnoxiously, his hip bumping hers every time he rocked his swing forward.

"Go away," she said.

Naturally, he grinned and moved closer. Maybe she should try negative reinforcement. If she demanded he sit in her lap, would he run toward the opposite end of the island?

"Not feeling friendly?" He made a face and yanked the lime out of the longneck the bartender slid over the counter. He took a long pull, the muscles of his throat working. Not that she was staring or anything, but ignoring Levi just wasn't possible.

"I'm not in the mood for your shit," she admitted.

"You want to talk next steps? Review the plan?" He leaned back against the bar, staring out at the beach. It was dark now, but there were plenty of stars visible in the sky and just enough light to make out the small waves washing up on the sand. If she'd actually been here on her honeymoon, it would have been perfect. Instead, she got Levi. Go figure.

"I've already got a plan." As if she'd leave something this important to Levi. "I checked with the manager. Told him we had some questions about our ceremony and needed copies of the paperwork. He's got the wedding coordinator coming in two days and he'll call the minister for us tomorrow."

Levi grinned at her over his beer. "In that big of a hurry to be rid of me, huh?"

"You really want to be married to me until death do us part?"

He threw up a hand. "You can stop right there. I've seen you with a gun."

She snorted. "You're the better shot."

Computers were her strength, but Levi could make shots that should have been physically impossible.

"I'm not planning on shooting you," he said dryly, but his eyes twinkled at her. And…was that a hint of a dimple in his cheek?

God. He could be so cute.

"That's my point." She took a pull on her own beer. "You wouldn't last a month at being married. In fact, I bet you wouldn't stick it out a week before you hit the road and ran."

He shrugged. "It would depend. Are you planning on being a good wife in this hypothetical scenario of ours?"

She saw red. "That sounds like code for putting out every night."

"At least." He grinned at her again. "In fact, since we're married, we should take advantage of each other."

"Right." She rolled her eyes. "Like you really want

to have sex with me after blackmailing me. That would be a new low, even for you."

He shrugged his shoulders again and then, shoot, his eyes lit up. "I'm up for it if you are," he taunted.

Even if he hadn't blackmailed her into coming with him, Levi's pretty package was wasted on her. He was the sexual equivalent of the loaner sweatshirt that got passed around when a girl was cold. Every female had had a piece of him, so no way was she sleeping with him, too. "No sex," she said firmly.

In addition, if it turned out that they really were married, she wasn't risking an easy annulment, so it was better to make her position clear now. Before she finished her cocktail and returned to their villa to deal with the one-bed-and-a-basketful-of-sex-toys situation. Mr. Manwhore might be the last SEAL on earth she'd sleep with, but she wouldn't put it past him to pursue her. He liked sex, and their ostensible marriage would put a crimp on anyone's style.

"Okay," he said agreeably.

Right. She snorted and he looked at her.

"Like you could go a week without having sex."

"I absolutely can." He sounded confident. She'd give him that.

She, on the other hand, was hyperaware of his long, powerful legs stretched out in the sand next to hers. He was still wearing his BDUs and combat boots, and for no particular reason, the sight of him ready for anything got her going. Or maybe it was just that he was a gorgeous, available jerk and she'd been without a boyfriend for too long.

"Pull the other one," she said dryly. "I've seen you in

action, remember, and going without sex while you're out in the field doesn't count."

"You think I'm going to cheat on you while we're married?" He managed to sound surprised, but it wasn't like he was the poster child for monogamy.

"We're not really married. Anything we do doesn't count." She wasn't sure she really meant that, but there was no point in setting herself up for disappointment with Levi.

"I keep my promises." He set his beer bottle back on the bar with a small click and leaned forward—*surprise*—to take her hand, his calloused fingers threading through hers in a rough-tender caress that was inexplicably good. His thumb found a sensitive spot in her palm and rubbed. Okay. Maybe *she* was the one who wouldn't make it a week.

Which was undoubtedly his point.

"I dare you," she blurted out, her mouth rushing ahead of her brain. "No sex for one week."

"Sure." He nodded agreeably. "You said the sex shop's closed, so no worries."

She'd never thought he would take advantage of their possibly married state. He wasn't that kind of guy. They were plenty clear on that particular point—it was just everything else they disagreed about.

"But," he said, his voice a low rasp. "If I take your dare, you take mine."

Her hand shot up. "No. I'm done negotiating with you."

Of course he kept right on talking as if she hadn't said anything. "For each night I go without sex, I get to choose a drink for you from Fantasy Island's cocktail menu."

She really, *really* needed to ignore the pulse of heat that suggestion generated in her belly. And lower. This was Levi. She didn't even like him, but apparently her body thought angry sex was something she should try at least once in her life. Preferably tonight.

He watched her calmly, but there was no mistaking the tension in his big body. He had her and he knew it. The problem with having worked with Levi in the field was that he'd learned things about her, like the way she responded to a challenge. Jesus. Emotionally, it made her feel like a five-year-old—when parts of her definitely were all adult around him—but she just couldn't walk away from a dare.

"You want to get me drunk?" Somehow, she didn't think he was talking about alcohol.

His teeth flashed as he snagged the drinks menu from the bar and waggled it in front of her. "We both know I'm talking about the other menu, babe. The secret menu, where the drink names are code for sexy stuff. *Pink Panties. Angel's Tit. Tie Me to the Bedpost.* I pick the drink. You do the deed."

4

THE EXPRESSION ON Ashley's face registered a whole lot of *hell no* and *you've got to be kidding me*. If he'd been any kind of gentleman, he'd have looked away. Seeing as how he'd moved into bastard territory long ago, however, he merely flipped the menu open and ran his finger ostentatiously down the list of cocktails.

Her long lashes flicked down, her brown eyes following his finger as a truly spectacular blush painted her cheeks. Special Agent Dixon wasn't a pretty blusher. No delicate shade of pink there. Her whole face flamed as though she'd been dipped in Day-Glo red. The color was kind of cute, actually, although he'd have bet his last paycheck that nothing shocked her.

He'd have lost that bet.

The corner of his mouth quirked up. Guess that won him points in this game of one-upmanship they were playing. He was actually capable of shocking snarky, no-nonsense, I-can-beat-your-ass Ashley Dixon. Today was a red-letter day, and he'd fucking mark it in his calendar. They'd worked together for the last year, and he could count the number of times he'd seen her look out of her element or anything less than perfectly confident. The woman was a chameleon, capable of fitting in anywhere and with anyone. She thought she knew the best way to handle every step of their missions. Worse, she'd been right. She pointed out her accuracy constantly and it was not an endearing trait.

"*Sex on the Beach, Screaming Orgasm, Bend Over Shirley.*" He winked at her. "Or should I substitute your name for that last one?"

Her blush got deeper. Any brighter and orbiting astronauts would be able to spot her cheeks from space. Together for less than twelve hours, and already he'd pushed her to Code Red. Provided he survived, this week together was turning out to be one of his better ideas.

She sucked in a breath, which undoubtedly meant she was about to start talking or yelling, and *that* was his cue to keep right on going. Once Ashley got started, she didn't stop until she'd won.

"Nothing to your liking, Dixon?" He gave her his most winning smile. "Let's try—"

"Shut up," she growled. He recognized the look on her face. If she'd been a fellow SEAL, they'd have been rolling around on the sand by now, trading punches. Still, her expression was priceless. He reached for his phone. A moment like this deserved to be immortalized.

"Jesus, Brandon. Have pity on the bartender. He's gonna think we're having marital problems already."

He thumbed on his phone and raised it. "Say cheese."

She slammed her hand down over his, pinning his fingers to the bar. With her other hand, she pocketed his phone.

He whistled. "Nice move."

If he were a lucky man, she'd kill him quickly. Since, however, he was currently married to Dixon and stuck on a tropical island after taking a vow of chastity, his luck was clearly nonexistent. Too bad about the phone, though, because the pictures would have been spectacular. He wiggled his fingers beneath hers.

"We're done talking," she snapped. Frankly, he was surprised she got the words out, because she had her teeth gritted so tightly she might need dental work. Her chest rose and fell beneath her shirt and damn it—was that a push-up bra? He leaned forward to get a better view. Why, yes, his cranky, ass-kicking wife was indeed sporting Victoria's Secret. His favorite kind, too, the type of bra that cupped a woman's breasts and laid them out framed in lace. He could run a finger down the deep valley her lingerie had created. Follow the path with his tongue and then his dick if he could sweet-talk her into a better mood…

"If you don't stop staring at my boobs, I'll hurt you." Her grip on his fingers tightened. Nice to know she'd been trained in hand-to-hand combat and interrogation techniques. He'd caught Mason teaching her a few new tricks, too, the last time they'd been on Fantasy Island. His fellow SEAL had claimed to be QAing the DEA's training program, but Levi was pretty sure the guy had just been stirring up shit. Dixon was mean. She didn't need *more* ways to hurt a guy.

Speaking of which…he pulled his fingers free. No point in leaving her with the opportunity, and they both knew she couldn't hold him if he wanted out.

"Is touching allowed? Good to know." Grabbing her hand before she could snatch it back, he turned it over and pressed a kiss into the palm. The way she dug her nails into his skin was plenty of answer. His Dixon was voting *no* on the touching. He wasn't playing fair, but boredom had to be the reason he'd started fantasizing about her underwear. He also wanted to kick ass, preferably beginning with the minister who had fake-for-real married them and ending with Gray Jackson, the SEAL lieutenant commander who'd brought them on the undercover mission to Fantasy Island in the first place. Not that Jackson had had anything to do with their not-so-*faux* beach wedding, but it was the principle of the thing.

"This is your fault," she huffed.

Like hell it was. He had no idea what specifically she was blaming him for now, but he'd deny everything to his last breath. That was his plan and he'd stick to it. "What's my latest sin?"

She tugged. He held on. "Our marriage. Our being stuck here on this island together. I'm busy, Levi. I have a life and I'm supposed to be preparing for a job interview next week. Flying down to Belize to sort out your screwup wasn't on my to-do list."

Wait. They were back to this *again*? "I get it. It's my fault."

Never mind that two people had to say *I do* to get married.

"You said *I do*," she bit out. "The minister asked you to say vows and you did."

"You did, too." He should know. He'd been there.

"You said it first. You were supposed to *pretend* to say the words."

"And we were supposed to have a *pretend* minister. So signals got crossed somewhere. We'll uncross them." He leaned back in his seat and motioned for the bartender. Another beer sounded like his safest bet at the moment.

The beach wedding had actually been kind of cool, although the costumes had sucked. Mason's sort-of girlfriend had rounded him up at sunset, claiming she needed a stand-in groom for a beach wedding shot for her blog. Since she was a professional blogger and photographer, the request had sounded legit—particularly since *he'd* known that the actual bride and groom had been detained by his SEAL team earlier in the week.

Since it was indirectly his fault that Maddie was in a bind, helping her out had seemed like the decent thing to do. Plus, Mason had definitely had a thing for the pretty photographer, which had been reason number two to lend an assist. Ashley had allowed herself to be sucked into the crazy, too.

It was hard not to like Maddie. She was cheerful and bubbly, her zest for living putting a smile on the faces of everyone around her. That probably explained Ashley's participation. Or maybe it had been her annual be-nice-to-strangers-and-nice-women day. Fuck if he knew or cared.

So maybe he'd said *yes* a little too enthusiastically when he'd been asked to participate. He also had a vague recollection of signing something that the minister guy had thrust in front of him. Confessing that the details were fuzzy probably wasn't wise.

One thing he definitely remembered about their wedding, however, was the clothes. Somehow, he'd always thought weddings involved big white dresses and dress uniforms. Turned out he'd been wrong. Wonderfully wrong. Ashley had arrived on the beach rocking a white string bikini with *BRIDE* spelled out in sequins over her outstanding ass. He'd offered to sound the letters out in Braille, she'd slugged him, and the ceremony had proceeded from there. If only they'd ended up not married, it would have been perfect.

"You still got the swimsuit?" Because truth be told, he wouldn't mind seeing it again.

"I'm ordering a new one," she said tightly. *"NEWLY DIVORCED."*

"That's a bunch of letters. Your ass is gonna need to get a whole lot bigger." Ashley had a great butt, curvy and apple shaped. Not that he'd ever been granted touching privileges, but he had eyes in his head and the sequins had screamed *look at me.*

She sighed, as though he'd screwed up yet again and it was killing her. "Are you telling me my butt looks big?"

He didn't think she'd misinterpreted his words that badly, but Ashley definitely liked to mess with him. "Stand up and I'll give you my honest opinion."

"You suck," she told him without heat.

"Imagine what I'll be like after fifty years of marriage." He grinned at her. "I'm like fine whiskey. I just get better with age."

"More like old produce," she muttered. "You stink and you're slimy."

"I'll put my trunks on. We can get some honeymoon shots. Or—" He grabbed his beer and discovered it was empty.

"Or what?" she asked impatiently, signaling the bartender for a refill for him.

"Or you could just strip my trunks off of me. I'm flexible that way." Coming on to Ashley Dixon, DEA agent and sometime-SEAL-team partner. Was that really what he intended? His dick was definitely up for it—she was a gorgeous woman—but his head also had zero problems with it. Betrayed on all fronts.

The bartended picked that moment to return with Levi's fresh beer. Ashley promptly swiped it. Apparently they'd already moved into the splitting-community-property stage of their breakup.

The bartender's head swiveled between them as he took in the tension. "Everything okay here?"

"See?" Levi snagged the beer and took a swallow. Since they were married, she could share. "Even the bartender thinks you're going to lose it."

Ashley made the teakettle noise again, the bartender beat a hasty retreat, and Levi mentally adjusted the guy's tip up. One of them needed to get something out of the situation.

"Murder is now a definite possibility," she growled.

He wasn't sure why she thought he was an ogre or Bad Marriage personified, but he hated it when she started slinging stereotypes around. Just because he'd never chosen to get married didn't mean he'd screw it up if he did. "If we're married, I'll fix it." He would, too.

Her eyes narrowed. "How? By killing *me*?"

And this was why they could never have a conversation. She was stuck on felonies and bloodshed.

"You're awful menacing for a newlywed on her honeymoon." He fought to keep his temper under control. So she'd been surprised by their newlywed status. He had been, too. Didn't mean she had to be a bitch about it.

"I've had provocation," she said darkly and knocked back his beer. Her throat worked as she polished off his drink and he made a note to order two beers in the future.

"And I paid for that," he said mildly.

She looked down at the empty bottle. "Sorry."

She wasn't. Not even remotely based on the satisfied smile she gave him, but that was okay. If she wanted a beer, he'd get her a beer. The whole reason for coming down here had been to take care of things. Dragging her along had been an impulse, but he still couldn't bring himself to regret it.

If they were married, he kind of liked the idea of having this week to themselves. It was no honeymoon, but it felt right. Almost as right as the unexpected urge to take care of her, which was stupid. Dixon was about as cuddly as piranha-cactus cross. She'd sooner cut his balls off than accept a helping hand from him. Honestly, he didn't see what the big deal was if he gave her an assist, but she'd always been funny that way.

"I'll fix it," he repeated. "You just tell me what you need."

She raised an eyebrow. "That's an open-ended statement, Brandon. You might want to rephrase."

Hell. Was he supposed to get turned on? Probably not, he decided, although he blamed her. *She* was the one who'd brought up sex in the first place. Not him. He was positively an angel. Really, he'd be doing her a favor to disabuse her of the notion that there was anything nice about him.

"I treat you to an island vacation and now you're giving me grief?"

She stared at him like he'd just crawled out of a foxhole after two weeks in the sand with no shower. "Is the word *romance* not even in your vocabulary?"

Sure was. He kept it in a list that included marriage,

peacetime and disarmament. Those were all good words—just not for him. He knew his limitations.

"I know how to romance a girl." The words probably would have sounded better if his voice hadn't come out all gruff, like her question was a challenge that pissed him off.

"Not sex her up," Dixon snapped. Jesus. Did she ever slow down and not take offense? Or was it just him that irritated her so badly? "I mean real, bona fide *romance*."

"Maybe you better give a *for example*. Are we talking flowers and candles, or do you want me spouting poetry?"

She snorted. "I'm not anti-flower, but that's not what I meant. You've got flowers and candles covered right here in this bar, and we're about as far from romantic as it's possible to get."

He made a give-it-up gesture with his hand. "You'd better educate me then, Dixon. As a public service."

"Tell me about the first girl you dated seriously."

"Gonna have to define *seriously*." Candlelight was a good look for Ashley. She smelled good—he'd noticed that as soon as he sat down. If pretty had a smell, it was Ashley. Fruit, flowers, maybe both. Hell if he knew, but he liked it. She smelled edible, and he wanted to lick her from head to toe, even though it would be a seriously bad idea. He had no doubt at all that she'd throttle him.

"Are *you* serious?" If her grip got any tighter on her beer bottle, she might shatter the glass. While he found her strength kind of sexy, he also found it frustrating. Her opinion of him was about as low as opinions could get. Kinda made him feel like he was the dog turd stuck to the bottom of her mental sneaker.

Whatever. Ashley kept right on yelling at him, which

was also familiar territory. "You dated the girl for more than a single night. You did things that did not involve a bed, a wall, the floor, or your penis poking her. You exchanged nonpornographic words, and if pressed, you could come up with a list of at least five things you liked about her that did not involve sex acts."

"You realize that, by that definition, we're dating seriously, babe."

Her forehead got the cutest little crinkle in it when she was thinking. Since his logic was solid, he tugged the beer out of her hand and stole a swallow. Beer always tasted better when it belonged to someone else.

"Arresting drug lords doesn't count as a date," she protested eventually. She knew he had her.

"I brought you to this gorgeous tropical island." He waved a hand around the beach bar. "You've got sand, stars, and unlimited alcohol."

Double gotcha.

She grabbed her beer back. "You don't like anything about me."

"That's not true either."

She pointed the beer bottle at him. "Prove it. If we're *dating*, tell me what you like about me."

"Might want to rephrase that, babe. Narrow your terms a little."

Honestly, he didn't know where Dixon had gotten the idea that he didn't like her. She was part of his team. He had nothing but respect for her job skills. So what if they rubbed each other the wrong way and gave each other shit? That didn't mean he didn't *like* her. Liking didn't come into it at all. The sidelong look she sent his way drove him crazy. Also made him want to misbehave, since she so clearly expected the worst from him.

"If you want an ode to your left boob, I'm happy to give it a shot," he continued. Yeah. That did it. Ashley's lips tightened, and her mouth flew open. She'd achieve nuclear detonation in three seconds if he didn't start talking fast. Since coming up with haiku about her breasts on the fly actually did exceed his capabilities, he gave her the truth.

"You've got killer skills with hardware. That's one. Two? You can break down and reassemble an M4 as fast as any of the guys on the team."

"Dating isn't a job interview," she said dryly. "And that's the kind of crap I put on my résumé. I'm not feeling the romance here."

"Shut up. I'm in charge of the list. Three? You're not afraid of anything. You got something to say? You say it. Doesn't matter if it's just me, or the SEAL team commander, or half of Congress. If it's on your mind, you'll say it."

She laughed. "Yeah. I'm blunt. I'll give you that."

He hadn't realized his list was up for discussion. "You're happy. That's number four. I've never heard you bitch about field conditions or wanting something different. Not saying you're Suzy Sunshine, but when we're on a job you don't bitch just to bitch. You roll with what life hands you."

She got a funny look on her face, but she'd started this. If she didn't like what he had to say, that wasn't his problem. And he actually *did* like her. So what if he'd never really thought it through before?

"Number five? I can hang out with you and drink a beer. Better yet, I can dare you to do stupid shit and you'll say yes. You've got a secret fun side, Dixon, and I definitely like that about you."

And conveniently, he knew just the way to do it, too. "So how about it? You taking my dare?"

THE LOOK ON Levi's face was pure mischief. No. Scratch that, because there was absolutely, positively *nothing* pure about the man. He was unashamedly filthy. Ordinarily, she kind of enjoyed that about him—not that she'd admit it—but he'd risen to the challenge and now he was proposing one of his own.

Performing a solo sex show wasn't on the top of her to-do list, however. Of course, making a personal sex tape or sending naked selfies wasn't on there either, so maybe she needed to loosen up. Or convince Levi to go first. There was definitely one thing they needed to get straight first.

"Wait." She patted the suggestive cocktail menu. "Some of these drinks are a team endeavor. I'm not having sex with you—or with anyone else."

Not that she was planning on losing the dare but, just in case, it was probably prudent to establish a few ground rules. God knew, Levi could probably have sex with an entire circus troupe, but she wasn't watching that, participating in that, or even *thinking* about that. Much.

He bumped her knee with his own. It was a good knee, hard and firm. She could feel the heat of his skin through his cargo pants and the sensation promptly sent her mind into the gutter. Darn it. It had to be the island and the anything-goes sexual ambiance that actually had her picturing Levi naked.

"Got it," he said. "Anything I pick has to be a solo act. No orgies, threesomes, or anything involving multiples."

Was she really going to do this? It was stupid. Juvenile. There were plenty of adjectives that covered the situation, and all of them screamed *stop and reassess*. She hesitated, the *yes* stuck on her tongue.

Levi raised a brow mockingly. "Chicken?"

"Don't be juvenile," she sniffed. She wasn't afraid of him. Or of losing. She'd seen the drinks menu—how bad could it be if she gave in?

Plus, who was she kidding? It was worth the risk just to watch Mr. I-can't-keep-it-in-my-pants SEAL suffer through a week of sexual abstinence. The odds of Levi's achieving an orgasm-free week were low.

"You're on." He toasted her lazily with his beer bottle. His *empty* beer bottle. Har. She'd won that one. "We've decided the rules for *my* part of the deal. Now let's finalize yours."

She concentrated on not hyperventilating while she got her thoughts together. Honestly, she had no idea how she'd gotten sucked into a sexy dare with Levi. Stuff just kind of happened around him, though, like he was a magnet for trouble. Maybe that had something to do with the fact that the man had never met a rule he didn't want to break. If the sign read "Don't climb," he climbed. She'd hung the equivalent of the world's biggest "Keep off the grass" sign on her chest with her celibacy dare, so maybe it was only natural he wanted to be all over her. Levi was perverse like that.

"I'm waiting," he said huskily, when she stared at him, lost in *those* thoughts. "If you've got sexy conditions, you might want to lay them on me before I'm old and gray."

It had been a while since she'd spelled out the conditions of a bet or a dare. In fact, the last time she could remember doing so was when she was all of twelve and egging her cousins on in a who-can-jump-off-the-highest-cliff contest. This wasn't much less juvenile.

"No O-face. No orgasm, with or without a partner or partners. Accidental orgasm still counts. And no hand action. You lose and you're voted off the island, effective immediately." She ticked the items off on her fingers. Reaching over, she patted him on the knee, her fingertips rubbing the hard, muscled warmth of his thigh. Wow. Brandon Boy was ripped. "You got all that, big guy?"

"That might be too much for me to process," he drawled.

"Use the big head, not the little one. You'll be fine."

He sighed. "Mean. I like that."

Maybe he'd lost his mind in that last foxhole. Or been too close to some kind of major explosion. From the way he grinned at her, her face radiated her suspicions loud and clear. "You're not supposed to *like* it."

"Babe, I'm going to win this dare. Tomorrow night is going to make it all worthwhile."

His middle name had to be *Incorrigible* and his next words proved it.

"I've got one question, though. Since we're laying down the ground rules. How are you going to know I haven't cheated?" He waggled his brows when he asked. God. She bit back a snort of laugher. "Are you volunteering to check?"

"For what? No. Don't answer that." She threw up a hand. "I don't want to know."

He shrugged. "Your loss."

Levi was actually kind of funny. Sure, the man loved a good fart or dick joke, but he wasn't mean. She hadn't meant it like that, but he was a good sport. She almost felt bad about his upcoming week of sexual abstinence, but it was probably good for him. A vacation for his dick before the damned thing fell off from overuse. Hanging out with him while they sorted out their marriage wouldn't be terrible.

When she stood up a half hour later to go back to the villa, he stood up, too. "At ease, sailor."

"If you're done, I'm done," he said, too affably. "The front desk only gave us one key."

Apparently he was still under the mistaken assumption that she'd happily share quarters with him. Confident, yes, but she'd straighten him out at the door if that was what it took. He didn't say much during the quick five-minute stroll back. The stars were out, visible overhead in a way they weren't back home. It was probably the lack of ambient light and Richmond traffic, but it was pretty. For once, Levi didn't say anything, which meant she could just enjoy the moment.

When they reached the villa, she double-timed it up the steps and turned to look at him. Levi had always had a thing about her giving him orders—or even suggestions—on their two shared missions. And by *thing* she meant *hated with a passion*. Her current position put her a couple of inches above the top of his head, which definitely worked for her.

"Good night, big guy." She motioned down the path. "Now that you've safely delivered your little woman, you can skedaddle."

"Nuh-uh. Not so fast." He bounded up the steps and rested a palm against the wall beside her head. He probably thought the move was sexy, and damn it, he was right. Hormones. That's all it was. Because he effortlessly tugged the key card from her fingers and tucked it into his pants pocket.

"Did you want something?" She gave him a pointed look. "Because the sex shop is closed and you're not sleeping with me."

"We're not having sex," he corrected her. "But I am planning on sleeping with you. We are married, after all." He flashed her a grin. Which was so. Not. Working.

Much. It wasn't working *much*. He was just trying to distract her with sex. Levi had always had a problem with being ignored. The quickest way to get a rise out of him was to pay him no attention. He was hot. He knew it. Of course, tonight it might also work to her advantage, since she needed to get her key card back and she had a dare to win. Two birds. One stone. Her path to victory was perfectly clear.

Opening gambit? Get his attention. Deliberately she stared at his mouth. "Levi—"

He didn't take his gaze off her face, but his thumb brushed over her bottom lip. Good lord, the man was dangerous. She'd need to up her game if she intended to win.

"That's my name."

His voice was hoarse. Another good sign. She leaned up and planted her mouth on his. The simple touch had her body heating up and her hormones going wild. Kissing Levi was like sticking her hand in the fire. No. Scratch that. It was more like jumping feetfirst into an active volcano. One of his hands found her hip, tugging her close. His other hand pulled gently on her hair as his mouth opened up for her. Her tongue swept into his mouth like the damned thing had a mind of its own and that was probably a good thing, because her brain had shut down at the first touch and someone needed to be thinking here.

Focus. She slipped her fingers into his back pocket and plucked the key card from its hiding place. And then, even though her girl parts were howling *traitor* at her, she ducked under his arm, opened the door…and slammed it in his face.

5

SINCE NONGENTLEMANLY BEHAVIOR had led to exile from the best mattress Levi'd ever lain down on, the logical next step was to try being a gentleman. Behaving was a new skill, but he'd survived BUD/S. In comparison, seven nights of marital bliss ought to be easy.

Levis scrubbed a hand over his face. *Ought* being the operative word. He'd led covert ops, spec ops, and dozens of undercover missions into hostile territory, but to be frank, this marriage business was all-new terrain for him. A smarter man would have made a few calls and gathered some intel. Two of his fellow SEALs were in long-term relationships with women they'd met on Fantasy Island. Either should have been able to give him the lowdown on being in a relationship without pissing off the female half. Possibly, his Dixon was an aberration. She certainly was unlike any of the women he'd previously dated. Of course, he'd never married any of those women, either. Hell, his former relationships had never outlasted the night on which he met, wooed, and won said women. Still, he genuinely *liked* women. He had plenty of female friends, and other female coworkers had refrained from killing him or issuing death threats on a regular basis. They even managed to pass out the occasional compliment. And seeing as how Dixon was very much of the female gender, her antipathy was irrational.

Wasn't it?

He shifted his weight and considered his options. She'd kissed him like she meant it, but her kiss had been a clever decoy. Probably he should work on his people skills, figure out how to convince Ashley to see things his way. She was stubborn as a mule, though, and he wasn't any better. The way he saw it, they were bound to clash so he might as well enjoy the sparks.

He let her disappear inside the villa, although he could have forced the door back open, could have held it open with a boot or kicked it down. But he was practicing his subtlety and Ashley definitely needed some space.

Which left him on the wrong side of the door.

He thought about that while he made a quick detour to the bar. Although he'd never admit this to her face, he actually kind of *liked* her. During the months they'd worked together, he hadn't made much of an effort to get to know her, and in hindsight, a part of him wished he had. Sure, he'd teased her, pushed her buttons. Meaningful conversation, however, had been nonexistent, although they had kissed that once. Strictly for business purposes.

He kind of liked that memory.

He and Ashley had been deep undercover, posing as biker and old lady. He'd been hanging out in a not-so-scenic alley behind a sleazy Sacramento bar, listening in on a gorgeous conversation about a truckload of semi-automatic weaponry due to arrive in NorCal at oh-five-hundred hours. That kind of hot information was gold. When Ashley had learned that he was in danger of being made, she'd joined him in the alley and he'd bolstered his cover story by kissing the hell out of her. She'd gone along with the kiss, and thanks to her, he'd looked like just another biker scoring some back-alley action.

Kissing her had been no hardship. She'd been all long, bare legs from her four-inch heels to the hem of a dress that barely skimmed the top of her thighs. And even though she'd disliked him intensely—and had, in fact, given him shit at every opportunity—she'd had his back that night.

She'd walked out of the bar, not stopping her sexy, hip-swinging saunter until she'd glued her front to his. Levi grinned despite himself. The things he'd done for his country, he deserved a medal.

The top of her dress had been even better than the bottom, barely there, the fabric molding her breasts and putting them on display. He'd trailed the back of one hand down her chest and patted her cleavage.

She didn't break cover, playing along as though she really was his old lady, but he'd figured she'd make him pay later for touching her boobs, after she'd put her plan into action. Ashley had always had a plan.

Her hands had gripped the back of his neck, as if she could hold him in place. She might not have had the muscle to do it, but he hadn't minded accommodating her. When she'd yanked his head down, he'd let her. Her mouth had covered his, her tongue declaring war on his lips and pressing for entry. Why the hell not? He'd opened up, and she'd swept in. Damn, but his

Dixon could kiss. She'd shoved her tongue deep into his mouth, exploring him in a no-holds-barred move that sent all the blood straight to his dick. He'd gripped her ass with his free hand, pulling her higher and tighter. She'd made a strangled noise when he notched his dick against her pussy, but then she got right back into it.

The not-so-nice part of him had wondered that night how far she'd go to save his ass. She might not like him, but certain parts of him apparently got a free pass. Or maybe they were frenemies now, and she just wanted to screw with him. Anything was possible with Dixon.

And then the door to the bar had opened a second time, and he'd understood the reason for Ashley's presence. The two bikers who'd stood there were the club's muscle. If they thought he'd overheard something, they were the fucking erasers who'd scrub his memories with their fists. The guys crunched over, not even trying to hide their approach. Levi had lifted his head and snarled a "Fuck off," like the only thing on his mind had been sex up against the wall.

And it had worked, too. The goons had left, certain they'd interrupted a back-alley tryst—but his cover had been intact. Ashley had made sure of that.

He'd had no idea she was such a good sport. Since he was a good sport himself, he snagged up a copy of the bar menu. He had homework to do. Their bet was kind of like being Jack—and he'd just been handed magic beans, which meant he needed to make his dares count. Or make sure no one cut down his beanstalk. Hah. She seemed to think he couldn't or wouldn't keep his dick in his pants, which was insulting. On the other hand, she'd handed him an easy dare to win, so he shouldn't complain.

Teaching Ashley a sexy lesson or two would be a pleasure.

The villa was good and dark when he returned. He debated knocking on the door—or just going to the front desk and getting a second key card—but where was the fun in that? Possibly he'd lost his mind, needling his not-so-sweet bride like that, but what was done was done, and he wasn't sleeping on the porch. Their goodnight kiss had been hot, even hotter than their first kiss. She'd opened up beneath his mouth, sexy and determined. And she hadn't stopped him, either. In fact, she had given as good as she got. Ashley always kept up in any contest, so it figured she'd turn their kiss into a marathon.

Slipping into the palm trees surrounding the villa, he worked his way to the stone wall around the outdoor bathroom. It took only seconds to pull himself up on top. Jesus. The resort definitely wasn't concerned about security. He dropped down silently on the other side. He hadn't seen much of the villas' interiors on his previous undercover mission on the island. Mostly he'd delivered towels in his guise as a pool boy, and staff quarters were nowhere near as plush as this bathroom. Guess that explained why his credit card had all but expired of heart failure earlier.

Moving silently, he crossed the bathroom to the door. The outdoor shower looked promising. Showering with Ashley could be fun. She'd worked her fingers into his hair during their all-too-brief kiss, and he'd like to return that favor. Fist her hair, pull her head back to the perfect angle for his mouth to hungrily claim hers. He groaned, feeling a sudden rush of heat in his groin. Fantasizing about her was probably a mistake, especially since she'd put having sex with him in the category of *last man on Earth*. Of course, their kiss seemed proof to the contrary, but he had no idea how Ashley thought. Getting him off could have been her next move in some devious game. Or her way of ensuring he lost his dare with her.

Perhaps he'd stride on into the bedroom and ask her. Imagining her reaction to *that* was enough to have him grinning again. She'd locked the door between the bedroom and the bathroom—maybe his easy breech of the outer perimeter wasn't entirely unexpected—but picking the lock took less than a minute. The door swung inward silently, and he moved stealthily into the darkened bedroom.

Ashley slept like the dead. She always had. Guess that was the difference between a SEAL and a DEA agent. The gun under her pillow was common ground, although the presence of the firearm would be hard to explain to housekeeping. He gazed down at Ashley sprawled in the middle of the four-poster bed, the covers pulled up around her ears, her sleek dark hair fanned out against the pillow. He had no idea how she could be cold in the tropics, but apparently she'd managed.

Which made it his husbandly duty to get in there with her and warm her up. He gave her another thirty seconds, counting down the time as he stared at the feminine mound under the covers. If she was playing possum, he'd give her ample opportunity to move on to the next stage of her plan. Ashley always had plans and next steps. Maybe she'd plug his ass with the cute little handpiece stowed under her pillow, or at least rip him a new one.

She certainly didn't bother sugarcoating her words.

He had a feeling that the day she actually said something complimentary to him would be a red-letter day—and that she'd mean every word. Good to have a goal, he supposed with a wry twist of his lips.

When she didn't budge, he deemed it safe to proceed. Stripping his clothes off, he dropped the lot by the side of the bed. When he was down to his boxers, he hesitated. Yeah. Best not to push his luck. Ashley was likely to knee first and ask questions later. Or do both. The woman could multitask.

Sliding a hand beneath the mountain of covers, he scooted her over. And hello, lucky night. The soft curves of her backside filled his palm. There was more to her than met the eye, and more than enough to hold on to. Still, since she hadn't actually invited him in, he finished shifting her and let go. She'd have to settle for sharing the bed, because his ass wasn't hanging off the edge of the mattress all night. Ashley mumbled something he wasn't entirely certain was English and then fell back to sleep.

He paused to consider his next move. He could stay on his side, all nice and orderly, or spoon her. She had to be cold if she was hunkered down under all those covers so…screw it. He crawled in and wrapped himself around her.

THE ENEMY HAD infiltrated during the night and Ashley's hormones were clearly happy to surrender. A large, muscled forearm was wrapped around her waist, the owner's hand brushing the bottom of her breast. Her tank top had worked its way down during the night, exposing her breasts, and when she inhaled her uninvited guest got a handful. Her right nipple was jealous of the left, since the tip rubbed against warm male fingers with each breath she took.

Or maybe she was dreaming, in which case she really, really needed to *not* wake up. Another five minutes of this, and she might come without Fantasy Man ever making it to third base.

The masculine snore in her ear was proof that she was awake. Her brain had more sense than to invite a dream lover who snored. And—she assessed the situation—hogged the bed. Judging by the light in the room, it was approximately the ass-crack of dawn, a guess confirmed by a bleary-eyed stare at the clock on the nightstand. Six in the morning. Even without rolling over, she knew who her companion was. Levi had an impressive set of scars on his forearm, plus there was zero chance of anyone else breaking into her villa when he was around. Even if he *hadn't* let himself in and made himself at home in her bed, he'd have been camped out on the porch on self-imposed guard duty. Once a SEAL, always a SEAL.

The man certainly wasn't easy to overlook—nor was the impressive erection tucked against her butt. The close contact must have short-circuited every last brain cell she had, because she actually took a moment to enjoy. Followed by a second moment and a third. There was plenty of Levi to appreciate.

She meant to drop-kick the man out of her bed so fast that his head spun, but instead, somehow, she wiggled back against him in a shameless move that felt damned good. Worse, the man did some kind of sliding thing that actually made her moan, which was the exact *opposite* of serving him an eviction notice.

Admittedly, it had been far too long since she'd had

sex of any kind. And it had been even longer since she'd had mind-blowing, toe-curling, hot sex. She was busy. Had a big job interview coming up. And she had a major corruption hearing to prep for. Those were all perfectly logical explanations for her lack of a sex life—and for why she was actually thinking about taking advantage of the hunky SEAL currently sprawled in her bed.

Even if said SEAL was Levi Brandon.

Her accidental, pain-in-the ass, temporary husband.

She could have sex with him, her libido suggested, and *then* kill him. After all, why waste a perfectly good SEAL?

"Brandon," she growled to drown out her baser impulses.

"Morning to you, too." He nipped her ear, and nerve endings she hadn't even known she possessed zinged to life. Why couldn't his reputation as the hottest US Navy SEAL stud ever to come out of Coronado be even a wee bit exaggerated?

"I don't recall inviting you to come in and make yourself at home."

"Nope," he said huskily, agreeable as always. She couldn't remember a time when she'd seen him angry. "But I'm a self-serve kind of guy."

She fought the urge to sink back into him. He might be self-serving when it came to letting himself inside the villa—and she'd be finding out exactly how he'd done that later—but he'd also be the kind of guy who made sure his partner had a darn good time. Her girl bits leaped to life, suggesting she put him to the test. Just once.

"Keep your penis to yourself," she snapped, reluctantly rolling away from him. Or trying to. His arm tightened, keeping her pinned in place.

He grinned down at her. "And here I thought you were checking to make sure I wasn't cheating."

"Not a chance in hell," she bit out. Her brain didn't get that memo, however. Oh, no. Her stupid, sex-deprived, overactive imagination immediately played her a full-color porn flick in which she slapped a hand on said penis. Squeezed. Ran her palm up and down the hard length until he was slick and they were both moaning. The fantasy was a little high school but God, it worked for her.

"You gonna spank me if I'm bad?" The rough rumble in her ear just made her melt further. Holy gods, but the man was trouble. From the smile in his voice, he knew it, too. There was a lesson in that.

"In your dreams."

"I do have great dreams," he allowed. She didn't need to see his face to imagine the grin stretching it. He was impossible. *Shameless* and *irritating* were two other equally apt adjectives that came to mind, but getting into an argument with Levi while they were sharing a bed was a recipe for disaster. Their arguments had always been heated, and her brain happily, gleefully reminded her of the one time they'd shared a little more than close proximity on a stakeout. He'd kissed her in the alley in back of the bar and she…needed to stop thinking. Attraction had always lurked beneath the surface of their encounters, and she suspected he knew it as well as she did.

"Why are you here?"

"You forgot already?" He nipped her ear again and that did *not* make her want to squirm. "Somebody demanded a divorce. I was just giving her what she wanted, because I'm such a giver."

"In. My. Bed." Levi had always loved to get her going. Not in the bedroom, but verbally. She'd say something, he'd counter, and before she knew it words were flying like tennis balls at Wimbledon, and the rest of the SEAL team had been captive spectators. She couldn't make so much as a simple statement about the weather without Levi turning it into a sexual innuendo.

He sighed dramatically. "Because you've got a mattress and I'm banking on Belize being a community property state, which means you have to share?"

Case in point.

"Belize isn't a state," she pointed out.

"Details. You're too damned picky." He bit her ear for a third time—although she had no idea why—and then rolled away from her. Right. But…was she really too picky? Someone had to call him on his crap, didn't they? And since he regularly said the most ridiculous things, it was practically a full-time job.

He bounded out of bed with cheerful good humor, the mattress shaking as he left. She'd forgotten how much she hated his early-morning perkiness.

"It's too early," she groaned, reaching for the pillow. If nothing else, she could drown him out. Or smother herself.

"Are you getting up? Or is that an invitation to join you?" Levi moved like a ninja. Somehow he'd made it around the edge of the bed and now stood over her, hands on his hips. At least he'd had the decency to wear something to bed—either that, or he'd collected his boxers on his round trip to her side of the mattress. The navy blue boxers hung low, exposing way too much SEAL for her peace of mind and highlighting ripped abs and an intriguing pair of hip bones. Holy God, the man had muscles. All sorts of delicious lines and ridges—and that was *before* she gave in to temptation and eyed his junk. Her Navy SEAL Ken had impressive…accessories.

He waggled his hips. Jesus. Had he gotten larger? Was that even anatomically possible? Because she was fairly certain he was already in the top percentile when it came to penis size.

"I'm happy to perform my husbandly duties. Just say the word."

She bet.

"Give it up," she advised, rolling over and burying her face in the pillow. No. No superspectacular, too-big-to-be-believed penis for her—especially when the penis in question was attached to one pain-in-her-butt SEAL. She must have been tired last night, though, because that was the only way a man that fine looking could have crawled into bed with her without *some* piece of her noticing.

A short, sharp smack on her butt had her lifting her head. She'd like to think he wouldn't dare, but this was Levi. There was *nothing* the man wouldn't do. If she was smart, she'd double-check the cocktail menu and make sure it contained no *Fifty Shades of Grey*-inspired drinks.

He rocked back on his heels and raised a brow. "Did you like that?"

"I'm not having this conversation now." Or ever.

Her refusal didn't stop her traitorous brain from immediately supplying an image of Levi spanking her. Her bare butt. His big hand rising and falling in a series of erotic slaps. Nope. No way. Kink was not her thing. She liked to be in control. So it was a big-time problem that, around Levi, she was *out* of control.

"Later?" He actually sounded hopeful.

His optimism should be illegal. She gave him a look. He could infer *when hell freezes over* for himself.

"If you're saving yourself for marriage, it's your lucky day," he said brightly.

"You'd make a terrible husband," she mumbled into her pillow.

There was a moment of blissful, wonderful, Levi-free silence. Since she didn't think she'd actually managed to hurt his feelings—the only sensations Levi seemed to entertain centered around his cock and his guns—she lifted her head. He stared back at her. Mr. Inscrutable had replaced Mr. Playful.

"The worst," he agreed, a shadow crossing his face. "I'd be awful."

For once, he didn't sound like he was joking.

"I'm not sure I'd be good at marriage, either," she admitted quietly. "My parents got divorced, and I'm really fond of my career. Maybe too fond. I mean, I'm not a commitmentphobe like you, but I'm in no rush to settle down either."

Levi made a rough noise, a sound she hadn't heard from him before. "I'm not afraid of commitment."

Apparently she could drive him crazy just by talking to him. Good to know. If the marriage turned out to be real and they couldn't score an easy divorce, maybe she could have him declared insane.

"Give me a for example of this much-vaunted commitment of yours."

He glared at her. "I'm a US Navy SEAL, babe. That takes commitment right there."

"Not to a relationship," she scoffed.

"The guys on my team are family," he said, and she believed him. He might not be into dating women long term, or marriage, but he'd made promises to the SEALs and he intended to deliver. If she hadn't been trapped in a fake marriage with him—a fake marriage she needed to undo ASAP before she jeopardized her own commitment to her career—she would have taken a moment to appreciate what he'd said. Her big, bad, playful SEAL had a soft spot. For his *team*.

"Maybe I've used up all my commitment being a SEAL," Levi continued. Apparently he was determined to hammer his point home. "So maybe that means I've got nothing left to give when I'm off the field. Most of the guys who try BUD/S drop off. That's not a slam on them, because it's a hard thing. You don't get in just by asking. You have to earn your spot in the training class, and then you have to earn it every single day thereafter. There's no easy pass, no shortcut."

"So you're married to the SEALs," she said. It made sense. He wasn't wearing a wedding ring, but he'd committed body and soul and he wasn't the kind of guy who shirked on a responsibility.

"We started out with a hundred and twenty guys in our class and six months later there were less than thirty of us. You have to be the right guy and it has to be the right job. I won't make a promise I can't keep, and I can't promise to be the guy who comes home after work, who hugs his wife and his kids, and who they can count on to be there. Because I'm busy being a SEAL."

Who had replaced devil-may-care Levi with this passionate, earnest soldier? Sometimes a strategic retreat was a girl's best bet.

"I call dibs on the bathroom," she announced and ran for the shower.

The faster they got their divorce, the better.

SHARING A BED with Ashley shouldn't have been any big deal, even after their awkward conversation the night before. Levi had bunked down in plenty of strange places, and with more than one team member. Limited space, enemy fire, temperatures cold enough to require the sharing of body heat—he'd done it all. It was all part of that married-to-the-SEAL-team thing.

So he'd had morning wood. He wasn't going to apologize for recognizing that she was one beautiful woman and a big improvement on his usual hairy, sweating, cursing teammates. Even when she was half asleep, hair standing on end as she threatened to cut his balls off. Her aversion to morning was kind of cute, and she'd calmed down when he'd fetched her some coffee after she'd finished her shower.

The wedding coordinator had agreed to meet with them at eight o'clock. While he appreciated the early time, he had to wonder if she'd misunderstood the purpose of their meeting, because she'd arranged to meet them in the resort's wedding chapel. The place was over water and was all light, airy shit with views of the surf and the lagoon below. At least the glass panels set in the floor guaranteed that if the ceremony got boring, guests had options.

He didn't recall meeting the coordinator during his previous visit. He was sure he'd have remembered someone so...*pink* was the only word he could think of to describe Ms. Megan Hartly. From the pink dress hugging her skinny body to the pink ribbons on her shoes and the pink nail polish decorated with some kind of sparkly pink flower things—the woman was a pinkapalooza. Hell, she probably pooped pink, and he couldn't begin to imagine the kind of weddings she organized.

She plunged straight into talking, not giving them so much as a second to explain their purpose in meeting with her. The weather, the shore, something the resort had recently done to the wedding chapel. An endless stream of blah-fucking-blah poured out of her mouth. Levi zoned out and let the words wash over him. She'd stop when she was done.

And sure enough, eventually the wedding coordinator skidded to a verbal halt and eyed the two of them. "How can I help you today?"

Ashley inflated beside him like a puffer fish. He was tempted to check her for spines, but he wasn't that stupid. She might have been staring at his dick earlier, but she hadn't been happy about her view—or his completely involuntary, purely biological reaction to her proximity and their shared bed. Which was all it was. So what if Ashley's morning grumpy was kind of adorable, and the way she'd glared up at him sleepily made him want to crawl right back in bed and find out if she enjoyed morning sex? It was Fantasy Island and he'd had a fantasy. Big deal.

Shoot. The wedding coordinator was staring at him, clearly waiting for an answer to her question. Normally this would be when Ashley took over, barking orders and "suggestions" that were actually more orders, just couched in slightly politer language. He slid her a sidelong glance and discovered her staring at Pink. She looked shell-shocked.

"Do you need more pictures? Do you want to re-create your special day? Vow renewals?" Pink looked expectantly between the two of them.

Ashley choked out a laugh and cut the woman off. "God. None of the above."

Prayer probably would help right now, but he figured the wedding coordinator definitely required them to spell it out in plain ole English, because the woman clearly hadn't gotten the memo about why he and Ashley were here. Explaining would be awkward as hell. Since Ashley looked like she was choking on her tongue, however, he guessed it was up to him.

"Ashley and I were here about three months ago. We helped a photographer friend out by posing for some wedding pictures and going through a fake ceremony."

The wedding coordinator blinked. "I can assure you, there's nothing fake about our weddings."

Yeah. Hearing that three months ago would have been awesome.

"That's precisely the problem," Ashley snapped. "We did not intend to end up married. Let alone to each other."

The wedding coordinator looked kind of like a rabbit facing down a snake. The poor woman knew she'd never win going up against Ashley when Ashley had that intent look on her face. Plus his "doting" bride also managed to make marriage to him sound as though she'd stepped in dog shit, so her unhappiness was abundantly clear.

"You got married…by accident?" The words clearly did not compute in Pinky's universe.

"Exactly," Ashley huffed. "We thought we were just posing for some pictures for a mutual acquaintance—not actually getting married. We didn't mean a word of what we said, and we were expecting an actor instead of a legitimate minister."

The ensuing silence stretched out a little too long. Yeah. Said out loud, the whole thing sounded shady to him, too. Levi took pity on the coordinator.

"How do we verify that we are, in fact, married?"

"And if we are, how do we end it?" Ashley added.

Her eagerness to get rid of him was damned unflattering, although it wasn't as if he wanted to be married, either. Most married SEALs he knew were on rocky ground at home. Years of war damaged a man. The guy would drink too hard. Struggle with posttraumatic stress disorder. Or bounce between anger and emotional numbness.

Sleeping six hours or more a night didn't happen anymore for most of them, himself included, and it didn't help that talking to a spouse about what he'd seen or done on a mission was off-limits. Add in spending eight to nine months a year away from friends and family, and the military life took its toll. His avoidance of the married state was actually a kindness.

The wedding coordinator tapped a pink nail against the binder she clutched to her chest. "You both were in Belize for three days prior to the ceremony?"

That was easy to answer, as long as the woman didn't need a detailed itinerary. Since he'd been on Fantasy Island on a covert op for Uncle Sam, he hadn't exactly been cooling his heels, but he'd done the time. He nodded. "We both were."

"Did you submit an application?"

Ashley perked up, clearly scenting an out. "Like fill out a form and sign stuff?"

The coordinator nodded. "That would have been typical, yes. It's a prerequisite for getting a marriage license. We can call the minister and he can verify which names were on the license."

It seemed unlikely, but maybe the guy had crossed off one set of names and penciled in another.

Ms. Pretty-in-Pink pressed on. "The Register General would have required proof of citizenship, copies of your passports, and someone to witness your signatures."

Ashley looked even more hopeful. "We didn't provide any of that."

No, but the original couple—the one he and the SEAL team had arrested for being part of a major drug operation—likely had. More and more, though, he had his doubts that he and Ashley were actually married.

"Someone mailed me a marriage certificate with our names on it." He produced the folded piece of paper and the coordinator scrutinized it. He could practically hear Pink's brain working overtime, trying to explain the total paperwork snafu. He imagined it wouldn't reflect well at all on Fantasy Island, if the resort went around accidentally marrying the wrong guests.

Ashley elbowed him. "Did you bring the *original*?"

Her confidence in him was stunning. Did she think he'd accidentally trip and send their certificate flying into the ocean—and that there would be no other copy in existence?

"I made a copy," he said shortly. Why couldn't she ever trust him to have her back?

The coordinator turned the paper over and studied

the back. Which was plain white, creased, and possibly sported a leftover piece of Snicker's Bar. Which of course Ashley noticed. She lived to give him crap.

"I can see you were super careful," she drawled, flicking the chocolate residue off the paper.

Levis flexed his jaw. He'd brought her the damn certificate, hadn't he? So maybe he hadn't had the thing framed, but she had it, and that was what counted. She could save the pissy look on her face for someone else.

"Walk me through the key points again," he said to Ms. Pink, ignoring Ashley. "And tell me what you need from us."

The coordinator looked uneasily at Ashley, as though she sensed Levi's bride was about to explode, but plunged into explanations. "Since you didn't fill out the application forms or provide proof of citizenship and identity, it's a question of whether you actually had a valid marriage license. If you did, the next question is whether or not your marriage was registered with the Registry Department. Since you received the certificate with your legal names on it, something happened somewhere, but I'm not sure it's enough to have the two of you married. The problem is that the Registry Department isn't open at the moment. Storm damage."

Pink gave a flustered wave apparently intended to convey the impact of a tropical storm on a building full of unprotected filing cabinets.

"There must be backups," Ashley said.

Having worked with her before, Levi recognized that what she really meant was *any sane person would have backups and I refuse to accept that you don't.*

Pink opened her mouth. A little squeak came out. Apparently, she was used to dealing with happy couples who were actually eager to get married, and Ashley didn't compute in her universe.

"Just find out," Ashley said in a clipped tone. "Quickly."

He had a feeling that *quickly* meant *before my job interview and the corruption hearing*.

"What happens if turns out the marriage is valid?"

The coordinator gave him a tight smile, clearly wondering if the next word out of his mouth was going to be *lawsuit*. "Then you could petition for an annulment."

From the way the woman was drumming her pink manicure against the binder, he was willing to bet that annulments were trickier than marriages.

"How long would that take?" Apparently Ashley had come to the same conclusion.

"Belize is a Catholic country." The coordinator shrugged, not done raining on their parade. "You would need to petition the Church, and that is not a speedy process. It would be much quicker to seek a divorce."

Levi got that the woman earned her living up-selling weddings, but she actually sounded cheerful as she pointed out all the obstacles.

"It's not easy to get divorced here, either," she continued. "But because the US recognizes foreign marriages, you don't have to obtain the divorce in Belize. You could do so at home. I'll get copies of the license and the application, and we can go from there." She shrugged. "But I'll be honest, I have no idea how your names ended up on the certificate."

"So maybe we're not married," Ashley said hopefully as they stepped outside. The jungle heat already had her shirt clinging to her skin. He got that she preferred the single life to him, but she didn't need to sound so cheerful about their situation.

"Maybe," he grunted.

"And if not, we'll get a divorce in Virginia." She heaved a sigh of relief. "I'm not touching your assets, so it should be quick and painless—unless you want a piece of my condo?"

Levis scowled at her. "You know I'm not touching your stuff," he said, resenting the implication that he'd take anything that belonged to her. Maybe he'd go touch base with the front desk, see if they could shed some light on where the marriage certificate had come from. He was pretty certain the envelope had been mailed by the resort.

"I can't go to my job interview married," she said.

"Why not?"

She gave him a look. "When I filled out the paperwork, I declared my marital status to be single. Committing perjury isn't going to endear me to the interviewing committee. Either I lied about being married, or I was careless about something really important." Sighing with frustration, she added, "At best, I look like an idiot. At worst, I look unethical and like I had something to conceal. Plus, most agents aren't married. How many SEALs do you know who get married and stay married? I mean, did you ever think about getting married for real?"

"To you?"

Yeah. That had come out all wrong. Crossing her arms over her chest, she shot him another look, even less flattering than the first. "To anyone who would have you."

LEVI DROVE HER NUTS. The man took nothing except the SEAL team seriously. Otherwise, life was one big, humorous game in the Levi-verse, and Ashley had no idea how she'd gotten swept up in his particular brand of crazy. Coming here with him had been stupid, except she hadn't trusted him to follow through on their marital problems.

"I hadn't thought much about it. I don't have a problem with it. How about you—*what*?" He made a mock-hurt face when she smacked him in the shoulder. "You asked me a question. I was just tossing the conversational ball back to you. You can't blame me for that."

"I can blame you for whatever I want," she informed him.

He sighed. "I've noticed that. And you still didn't answer my question. Is there a Mr. Dixon—other than my fine self—on your horizon?"

She was all about her career—and so was he, if they were being honest with each other. And she knew he wasn't asking because he had a genuine desire to hear her answer. He was more *how can I piss Ashley off?* than he was *let me get to know my dear wife intimately and genuinely.*

"My job isn't to find The One. It's to put the bad guys out of business. I don't need a man in my life when I can protect myself, both physically and financially."

"That works for you?" He sounded genuinely curious.

She shrugged. "I'm not worried about being labeled a bitch. I like to eat, I need to work, and any Mr. Right who feels intimidated or traumatized can take a long walk off a short pier."

He nodded, as if her revelation was perfectly understandable—or just background noise. Was he even *listening* to her? Instead of responding, he made framing motions with his hands, and once again she had no idea what he was thinking. With the exception of the sexual innuendoes that he tossed out on a regular basis—and she understood those just fine, unfortunately—the man's thought processes were a mystery. Maybe he didn't think at all. Possibly he acted on impulse, led by his dick and his seemingly unquenchable need to screw the greater part of the female population and…he made another one of those stupid hand gestures. It wasn't American Sign Language, nor was it remotely intelligible.

"What?" She gestured impatiently toward his hands. Would it kill him to use his words? "What's that supposed to mean?"

"I'm trying to imagine you in one of those big white dresses."

Well, he could imagine away because hell would freeze over first. "I'd never be that kind of bride."

Now he grinned and she didn't need any words to know what he was thinking. For crying out loud, did the man think about *anything* besides sex?

"Stop it." She punched him in the stomach, which felt like slamming her hand into a brick wall. A sexy, cut wall wearing a wicked grin.

The grin got wider. "You got mind-reading skills now?"

Yeah. That wasn't a denial.

"You might as well tell me." She didn't manage to hold back her sigh, but that had to be better than cursing the man out, right? And Levi, being Levi, didn't hesitate to fill her in.

"I'm imagining peeling one of those dresses off you. Or getting underneath it. We could play honeymoon."

Yeah. Like *that* was happening. A traitorous thrill shot through her at the thought.

"One-way ticket off the island," she reminded him. "You lose, you pay."

He flicked her a quick salute. "Yes, sir."

After that he was blessedly silent until they arrived back at their villa. She wondered if he was going to follow her all over the island like a lonely puppy, or if he could be convinced to go do his own thing, whatever that was.

"Go away," she told him. "I've got work to do."

The corruption hearing alone required hours of research and careful planning. If she just showed up and answered questions blindly, the panel would skewer her.

He smiled agreeably, but slapped a palm on the door when she tried to shut it in his face. Again. "You're holding my clothes hostage," he pointed out. "Lock me out and I'll be forced to go naked."

"In that case, please do come in." She gestured toward the room with a flourish. "And spare the female population."

He laughed, but moved past her. He confused the hell out of her. The meaner she was to him, the more he seemed to like it. Maybe he had some sexual wire or other crossed in his head. Good lord. For all she knew, the man was a closet sub in the market for a new dominatrix to rock his world.

She chewed on that while he rummaged in his duffel bag, coming up with shorts and a T-shirt instead of whips and leatherwear. Nope. Levi was the most take-charge man she knew, and in no universe could she imagine him taking orders from anyone other than his commanding officer…and even then, she had a feeling orders might be optional. Or more a suggestion.

"Dropping my pants now," he announced cheerfully. "Look. Don't look. It's up to you."

For the love of God. Grabbing her laptop, she dropped down into a chair and flipped the lid open. When he dragged his zipper open, she did not look. Or peek. Or even *think* about what Levi might be doing. She kept her eyes dutifully glued on her laptop screen. The hearing transcripts ought to be a total passion killer.

"Chicken," he drawled, as if a simple one-word insult would be enough to make her turn around. So he was hot. She didn't need to look to know it. Instead of ogling her captive SEAL, she needed to use her downtime to her advantage. She had that hearing about the Central American incident to prep for. Plus, in addition to formulating possible answers, she needed to check in on work. Just in case anyone missed her.

"I'm going running," he announced, completely unnecessarily in her opinion.

"Go." She waved a hand toward the door.

She'd never been fired, never failed to get a promotion or win. This suddenly married business, however, was like running down the mat toward the vault and realizing as your foot came down that someone had tossed a banana peel on the mat. And it was silly and stupid and inconsequential…but your heel was sliding anyhow, and there was every chance you'd slam into the vault instead of hurtling over it.

For the next couple of hours, she kept her head down, immersed in her work. Levi had left shortly after she'd ignored his striptease, presumably to get a run in. Whatever. He could run back to the Belizean mainland for all she cared, as long as it kept him out of her hair and her life.

Given her last-minute request for vacation time, she'd agreed to work remotely when needed. Since she was offshore, it was also an excellent time to take another go at finding security flaws in her latest software assignment. She had some new ideas on how to hack through the firewall, and now was a great opportunity to test her theories. The covert ops work had been different and a chance to push herself, but coding was where she excelled.

And the icing on her work cake was that since she needed to go straight from Fantasy Island to the hearing about the Central American contretemps, she'd planned on using the downtime to prep for her upcoming job interview. She'd researched the position and drawn up a list of questions, but she wasn't a mind reader.

She'd already passed the medical requirements before, so she didn't anticipate a problem there. And even though she'd made the candidate list sent to the Career Board, the job simulation worried her. Because the truth was, if they did another background check, she didn't know how her maybe-marriage to Levi would read. She hadn't disclosed it on her application since she hadn't known about it but...

Stupid wasn't an excuse.

Some time later, her phone buzzed, alerting her to an incoming text message. Still lost in the code scrolling across her screen, she grabbed it and thumbed through the messages. Apparently Levi had decided to revert to his teenage years. A picture of his butt in his wedding shorts flashed across her screen. She'd remember those shorts to her dying day, because the word GROOM had been bedazzled across his gorgeous backside. Apparently, he'd kept them as a souvenir.

Proving my point you're an ass, she texted back.

Not that he cared about her opinion, but surely the man had to know that anything he posted on the internet could and would be held against him. He did have a mighty fine butt, though. And an unquenchable zeal for texting. Throughout the afternoon, he texted her new pics of himself in the shorts. After he'd covered all the angles, he'd started covering up one letter or the other, spelling out different words. ROOM. OO. GOO. While beating him at Scrabble looked likely, she had to hand it to Levi. He had no problem turning his sense of humor on himself.

When he popped the door open later that afternoon, the shorts weren't in evidence. It was almost disappointing.

"I sort of thought the *leave me alone, I'm working* was implied," she muttered. "I told you to go away."

He grinned at her and rocked back on his feet. "I went. Now I'm back. I'm proving I can be trained."

"Like a dog," she said sourly, head still lost in her code.

He barked, and she smiled despite herself. Okay. So he was kind of cute. *And annoying.*

He came over and leaned his hip against the desk where she was working. If he was trying to distract her, it was working. Levi's front view was as spectacular as his back view. Plus he'd once again lost his shirt somewhere, so her nose was inches from a very impressive six-pack. The way he nudged her laptop screen was less attractive.

"Don't touch my stuff." She saved her work, however, starting the remote backup process. Things tended to get blown up, broken, and otherwise borked around Levi. That might be helpful on a mission, but it was hell on hardware.

"You need to get up and move." She opened her mouth and he pressed a finger against her lips. "The bathroom doesn't count."

Busted.

He pushed the laptop lid down a few inches, a devious gleam in his eyes. "Come for a run with me."

She steadied the lid. "You screw up my backup, and…"

"And what? You'd have to catch me first, in which case you might as well get up now."

She sighed ostentatiously. "You do realize that DEA agents don't sit around all day, right? If you run, I'm trained to catch you."

"Uh-huh." Dark eyes flickered down her body and heat washed through her. "I'm bigger."

"Doesn't make you faster." She shoved to her feet. Guess it was up to her to teach her SEAL a lesson. Sure, he'd outrace her, but she could definitely make him work for it, plus she wasn't above cheating in a good cause. "I'm good."

"I'm better," he said. The man definitely didn't have a confidence problem.

She changed into her running clothes—in the bathroom because Levi refused to budge from their room and she refused to give him a peep show—and then headed outside. She walked the first quarter mile, warming up her muscles and stretching out the kinks. She hated to admit it, but he was right. She'd have worked away the night, and she was already stiff.

Becoming a DEA agent had required passing the Physical Task Test. The PTT had been partly about acquiring the necessary muscle mass and partly about discovering the necessary mental toughness. Pull-ups, sit-ups, push-ups, running—that was the easy part. Practice made perfect, didn't it?

Basic Agent Training at Quantico, Virginia, had meant more than banging out reps, however. She'd been screamed at, yelled at, and all-round abused. So whatever Levi dished out, she could take. She was used to being the girl on the team and winning that particular uphill battle. Because she *only* played to win.

When they reached the trail edging the beach, she didn't bother giving him any warning, just took off running. He fell in beside her. The birds in the palms made more noise than a mariachi band. The air was heavy and humid, the sun turning the water pink and red. The last time she'd been here, she'd been focused on the mission and staying in character. There hadn't been time to simply drink in the lush, tropical surroundings.

When the trail looped back, she looked over at Levi. "Race you."

Then she took off like a shot. He snagged the back of her T-shirt, slowing her down. She elbowed him in the ribs. When the beach and their stuff loomed up in front of them, she put on a spurt of speed, sprinting for all she was worth. She could hear him pounding behind her, closing the distance too fast.

He took her down to the sand, tackling her and rolling to take the brunt of their fall. Too bad for him that she was ready for that trick. Flinging out her free hand, she tapped the pile of towels first.

"I win." She wriggled, but he held her fast, her back

glued to his chest and her butt firmly planted over his groin.

"You cheat."

"Do not."

He grunted and his arm tightened briefly, then he let her go. She rolled off him and flopped on the sand beside him.

"I'm competitive," she admitted, poking him in the side with her elbow.

"Tell me something I don't know," he said, and nudged her back.

"I did competitive gymnastics for eight years."

His head tilted. "Really? With the leotards and the sparkle stuff on your face?"

"I was good," she informed him.

She had been, too. Had thrived under the pressure of only getting one chance. One chance to hit on the vault and win. No matter how many times she got it right in practice, the only vault that counted was in competition. No mistakes were allowed. You started with a perfect score, and the judges took away points for each mistake. She hadn't been in it to win—she'd been in it not to lose.

"Why'd you stop?"

"I stopped winning. I jammed my knee one too many times and my boobs got too big and got in the way." She shrugged. "Sometimes it's just time to move on."

"You don't like losing," he accused, a mischievous glint in his eyes.

She shrugged. "Who does? Winning was the only thing I was ever good at."

"You know what this means?" He jerked a thumb at the horizon.

She squinted at it. Nothing particularly spectacular stuck out. No green flash, no invading army, no drug dealers skimming over the lagoon toward Fantasy Island. "That you suck at making conversation?"

"You're just too sweet to me," he drawled. "But that wasn't the compliment I was angling for."

"If you want compliments, you should find yourself a different wife."

The muscles in her abdomen burned. Working out with Levi had pushed her. He had more muscle mass than she did, and ran a much faster mile. Keeping up with him had been a good challenge.

He rolled to his feet, and she looked up at him in surprise. "Are you quitting?"

"Is everything a competition to you?" He looked genuinely interested in her answer rather than judgmental.

"Pretty much." She shrugged and knocked out one more sit-up. "I'm not good at losing."

The truth was, she *never* lost. She'd worked hard for her body, and the further she got from her teenage years, the more work it required to maintain the levels necessary to pass the DEA physical. If a workout didn't leave her drenched with sweat and shaking, it was a waste of time. Pushing harder and further had gotten her through the police academy as a girl and then through the DEA's training program because her rule was to never, ever, take the easy way out. If the mission called for running five miles, she sprinted ten. She gave it her all and therefore she finished first, fastest, best. If he didn't like that, tough.

Somehow looking at his ripped, muscled body, however, she thought he understood. He pushed himself, too.

"Better learn fast," he advised.

"That's sweet of you."

"One night's up—you owe me a drink." Oh, he was sneaky. He also looked pretty pleased with himself. Too bad that state wasn't going to last.

"Twenty-four hours. Time's not up yet."

"Cheater." He ran a thumb down her cheek. "You're a filthy, rotten cheater, Mrs. Brandon and it's time to pay up. You lose. I win."

6

"I AM NOT a cheater." Ashley gave him a repeat of the same incredulous look she'd shot him during the five-minute walk from the beach to the villa, and from the villa to the bar. Apparently making good on their dare was impossible in stinky workout gear. Whatever. She could pay up naked or wearing a toga for all he cared.

"The lady doth protest too much." Levi had no idea if she was denying their marriage or reneging on their bet, but she'd followed him and that said something. He snorted. As if he'd let her renege on a dare. She knew better than that. Stupid dares were practically the currency of their SEAL team, and it wasn't as though he'd twisted her arm to get her to agree.

"Don't mangle Shakespeare," she muttered, looking unhappy. Right. She hated losing. She never lost. Making her eat those words was going to be so much fun.

"I'll start you off easy," he said, because he was feeling magnanimous. "Sit."

"Hah-hah." She gave him a petulant look.

He nudged the seat next to him in a not-so-covert suggestion. Since the beach bar had swings instead of the usual stools, the wooden seat smacked gently into the general vicinity of her knees. Not that he could tell, given that she'd wrapped herself up in a gigantic muu-muu masquerading as a dress. He squinted. Or maybe it was a leftover tent from his last covert op, although bright pink wasn't the Afghans' color of choice. Made it too easy for the snipers to find. He half expected her to flounce away, but instead she parked her butt on the seat. Holy shit. He couldn't remember the last time she'd taken a suggestion from him.

When they'd gone undercover on the island, she'd dyed her hair goth black and punked out. That Ashley had rocked a neon-pink string bikini. Despite the crazy clothes, she'd been drop-dead gorgeous. The long pink thing she was sporting now had to drag in the sand when she walked, but the excess fabric was heavy and that was an unexpected bonus because the weight tugged the front low in a pretty spectacular display of cleavage. Little twisted braids of ribbons crisscrossed her tanned shoulders. One good nudge and she'd pop free.

She propped herself up on the bar and looked significantly at the menu by his elbow. "If you insist."

Hell, yeah. "You think I'd pass up this opportunity?"

She made a face. "No pictures. No sharing on social media. And no public spectacles."

The public spectacles caveat hadn't been part of their original bargain, but he could hardly blame her. Humiliating her also wasn't part of his plan. Having some fun? Yeah. That he was definitely up for, but he also felt curious—and more than a little horny. How far would she go?

With a dramatic sigh, she nudged the menu toward

him. "I want it on record that I'm a good sport. And that you cheat."

If Ashley was going to perform a sex act of his choosing, he could afford to be gracious and let the cheating accusation pass. He ran a finger down the menu and pretended to read the list of drink names, even though he'd decided earlier in the day which cocktail he was choosing. He didn't have to be mean about this, plus there were some things he wasn't sure *he* wanted to see. How would a woman like Ashley portray *Leather and Lace*, for example? He'd be an idiot to hand her a weapon like that.

While he read, she swung gently back and forth. Somewhere between the villa and the bar, she'd lost her shoes and was barefoot, her toes curling into the sand. She had cute toes, too. She'd painted her nails blue with white polka dots, and she didn't often do that girly stuff. He knew Ashley worried about fitting in with the guys. She was a woman in a man's world, and that had to be a challenge. But she'd always kept up, always given as good as she got. She was a good team member and he was proud of her.

"You'd have made a good SEAL," he told her, motioning for the bartender. The bar was nearly empty, with just one other couple on the far side. The pair were bent over a camera, flipping through their vacation shots. Hell, they practically had the place to themselves. *Perfect.*

She snorted. "The Navy hasn't encouraged women to do BUD/S."

Which was stupid, in his opinion. "They should." Female biology might not be up to some of the SEAL training exercises—he couldn't imagine Ashley hoisting a two-hundred-pound log over her head for hours on end—but missions weren't always about brawn. Brains counted too, and Ashley was strong in plenty of ways.

When the bartender came over, he didn't hesitate. "I'll have two *Silk Panties*."

The bartender didn't so much as blink. Good man. He just tossed out a "Very well, sir," and beat a retreat.

Ashley laughed. "I can't believe you just said that out loud."

"Are they going to revoke my man card?" he asked in mock horror. He wasn't the person who was going to be wearing the panties, after all.

"Silk panties are going to require a swim back to the mainland." She flicked her straw at him. "Because I'm cotton all the way, baby."

He opened his mouth, but she'd won this round. He was almost certain he made a sound halfway between a grunt and a moan. His brain had no problem mentally imagining her in a selection of Victoria's Secret's raciest, but the insta-boner in his pants told him that fantasizing was a mistake. Her gaze flicked to his lap, taking in the blatant evidence of his interest in her panties, and a wicked smile crossed her gorgeous face.

"You're in danger of losing the dare," she advised.

Hooyah, but she was right. "You lost tonight," he pointed out. "And I picked a drink."

"Silk Panties." She nodded agreeably. "I'm fairly certain most of the island is now aware of your order. I'm also sure you've got something in mind, so feel free to spill."

Jesus. "We're gonna trade. My panties for yours."

She stared at him like he was crazy. "In your dreams."

Hell, yeah. Pulling a pair of silk panties out of his pocket, he slapped the scrap of fabric ostentatiously on top of the bar. Preparation was his middle name tonight. He'd made a strategic pit stop at the resort gift shop earlier in the day. Dixon's new panties might be pink silk, but they were also of the thong variety and rocked some kind of sparkly pink-and-white zebra print never seen in the wild. They were awesome.

"Put those away," she hissed. "We're in public. See that couple over there? They're an audience I'm not entertaining."

He glanced obediently over at Vacation Picture Couple, who were still heads down over their camera. Was their possible attention her only objection? Because he'd anticipated more than one complaint.

"Nuh-uh." He nudged the silk toward her. "You get to put them on. You're fortunate. I could have ordered a *Dirty Silk Panties*."

In case she didn't get the idea—although she'd been dressing herself for at least two decades, so she had to know how the process worked—he picked up the panties and held them out in front of him. She eyed the expensive lingerie in his hand as if he'd offered her a snake. "God. Tell me they're new, at least."

Even he wasn't that much of a pig. "I went shopping just for you, Dixon. You should say thank you."

She caught her breath sharply, grabbing the panties and dropping them into her lap as the bartender came back. Levi had to hand it to her. Her timing was impeccable, as always. When the bartender slid the drinks in front of them, however, he had to question his choice. Jesus. The thing was pink. Very, very pink and served in some skinny flute with berries floating on the surface.

"What's in this?"

"Vodka, peach schnapps, and raspberry liqueur." Which explained the red berries.

He grabbed the flute, waited until the bartender had moved back to the other end of the bar and saluted Ashley with the drink. "You first."

She eyed the berries but didn't make a move to grab her glass. "You've drunk your own piss in a foxhole. You think this is an improvement?"

He was powerless to stop the slow grin from spreading over his face. "At least it comes in a glass."

Her head tilted, as though maybe the drink would look better from a different angle. "No one said I had to drink what you ordered."

Nope. Just act it out.

Because there was no point in wasting a perfectly good drink, he took a cautious sip. It actually wasn't bad.

She shook her head, looking amused. "You're unbelievable."

"Why?" Knowing Ashley, she had a dozen reasons, ranked from least to most important.

"I'd forgotten how much you enjoy sugar."

Yeah. So sue him. He took another swig. A *Silk Panties* definitely improved on further acquaintance. "And you're procrastinating. Put 'em on."

ASHLEY KNEW BETTER than to make a bet with a SEAL. You played, you paid. The guys were better than the Mafia at collecting. Levi slouched on his swing, one big hand wrapped around the fragile cocktail glass as he waited for her to grab his panties and…do what? Strip? Launch into some kind of porn show revue for the entire bar? She wondered briefly why the frothy pink drink only made him look more masculine and then gave up. This was Levi. The man was sexy to the bone.

He was also looking at her as if he expected her to run screaming. How typical. Did he think she'd never had sex? Granted, she wasn't in his league. If even half the rumors were true, the man had dropped his pants for ten, thirty, or possibly hundreds of women. She wasn't one to judge, but he simply didn't have a reputation for being discriminating. And that was the only advantage she had. If he thought putting on a show for him would embarrass her, she'd show him a thing or two. Standing up, she grabbed his drink. Liquid courage couldn't hurt.

"That's mine," he said good-naturedly. Now that she thought about it, she'd never seen Levi lose it or get angry. Maybe he performed secret SEAL missions with the same upbeat insouciance.

"Cheers." She took a hefty swallow of his cocktail and it was every bit as sweet as she'd expected. Good lord, she had no idea how people drank this stuff.

Levi made a little hurry-it-up gesture with his hand. "Don't make me order a second round. You won't like what I pick."

"You picking *Spank Me, Shirley*?" Hah. That was a point for her. Levi's eyes flared before he got himself under control. It was a good thing she'd gone with the maxi dress, because there was nothing more awkward than getting caught in a miniskirt with your panties around your thighs. She did a quick scan of the bar, but the resort was nowhere near full capacity, and the bar's occupants consisted of the bartender and one other couple. If she was careful, they'd never know.

And if she got busted? Well, she could drop the hem if her dress. Fast.

Mentally whistling a little show tune, she eased her dress upward. Ankles, calves, knees…it wasn't like Levi hadn't seen her legs before. She hadn't factored in a few key differences, however. Unlike their previous semidressed encounters, he was staring at her now with avid interest. And was that…heat glimmering in his eyes? Huh. It was kind of strange to think that Levi might be genuinely interested in her.

"You take much longer," Levi drawled. "And you're looking at a Class B felony stateside for public indecency."

Since she sincerely doubted anything she did could possibly shock or offend him, he had to mean the bartender. Shoot. Had he caught her? When she looked over her shoulder quickly, however, the man was still busy on the far side of the bar.

Killing Levi moved to the top of her to-do list.

"He can't see anything," Levi said in a low voice. "Yet."

As if Levi cared. He wasn't the one putting on the show. Still, the sooner she gave him what he wanted, the sooner this spectacle would be over. She hiked the dress higher. Ran a palm over the smooth skin of her inner thigh. She'd always liked her thighs. She ran regularly, so she had a clearly defined line of muscle, but they were soft and curved outward at the top just a little. She didn't have to be a skinny thing to get a guy's attention. Sure enough, when she trailed her fingers upward, Levi leaned forward like a fish on a line. Funny how a little skin could bring him to his knees.

"You're thinking something." Levi sounded hoarse.

"I like my thighs," she admitted, extending one bare leg. Her toes brushed Levi's thigh, and she decided *why not?* She set her foot on him and the skirt fell back. Her own panties were on full display now, and they might not be pink silk but they were definitely fabulous. White didn't have to be boring.

Levi made a rough sound, and a Cheshire-cat grin spread across her face.

Her SEAL liked the view.

"Too bad you took a vow of celibacy." She trailed her fingers higher. "But I sure didn't."

She threw a glance at his crotch. Despite the bar's relative darkness, there was no mistaking the impressive ridge beneath the front of Levi's fatigues. *Take that.*

"Not my best decision," he agreed thickly, but he didn't look like he minded all that much. She'd have to change that. The man needed to suffer. When she leaned in, she caught his scent. Bay rum and something foresty. It was kind of nice, really.

"Hold these for me." She dropped the silk panties onto his lap. Really, the man had no taste.

Sliding her foot off his leg, she reached beneath her dress and hooked a finger in her panties.

"I don't suppose I could convince you to lose the dress?" He leaned back in his chair, his hands loose on his thighs. She'd give him credit. He didn't *look* like he gave a damn.

She gave a soft laugh. "Not a chance in hell."

Her best bet—hah—was to keep teasing. She wriggled and gave a little tug. Her panties slid down her legs, the white cotton fluttering around her ankles. Not a flag of surrender, though. Nope. She preferred to think of it as throwing down the gauntlet. If she had to strip in public, Levi got to suffer, too.

She held out her hand. "Give them to me."

"I'm not sure this is what I had in mind."

"Too bad." She flashed him a smile. "Because this is what you're getting."

The pink drink was working nicely on her nerves now, the alcohol cocooning her in a warm glow. What if the casual pose wasn't actually a pose? What if Levi genuinely could care less that she'd dropped her skivvies at his command in the middle of a very public bar? Her body was tight and hot, her stomach liquid with something that was part embarrassment, part lust. Good lord, but she was turned on. She stepped out of her panties, not trusting herself to say anything.

"Ashley." He growled her name and the temperature on her internal thermometer ratcheted up another few degrees. The man had no business being so sexy, particularly when she got the feeling it was completely unintentional on his part. Levi just exuded SEAL hotness like it was part of his job description. Maybe she'd just gone without sex for so long that she was misreading his cues.

"You gonna look at me?" The laughter in his voice had her narrowing her eyes. Darn him. But she wasn't backing down, not when she'd come this far, so she stared him square in the eye.

"What?" She'd been afraid she'd see…what? Boredom. Laughter. She honestly had no idea. But Levi simply looked riveted. His casual pose wouldn't fool anyone now. He slouched on his seat, big, brawny arms resting on his thighs, but every inch of him was focused on her.

He handed her the silk panties. Before she could

react, he'd swiped up her abandoned white panties from the ground and tucked them into his pocket.

"Souvenir," he said, and winked when she made an outraged sound. Or possibly a squeak. Because she was closer than ever to pushing the man down to the sand and having her way with him. Which was still a very, very bad idea and absolutely not happening. Plus she had other things to worry about besides getting his penis inside her and possibly sand in some uncomfortable places.

First and foremost, she wasn't letting her panties end up on eBay or some other equally embarrassing spot. Like her office door or the windshield of her car. "You're supposed to buy postcards or commemorative spoons. Maybe a T-shirt and a wind chime. Give them back."

Naturally, he ignored the hand she held out. "I bought you new ones."

Uh-huh. She held up his panties, before remembering that *discretion* was her plan for the night. All those sequins might blind the bartender. "I like mine better."

The cost per inch of fabric had to rival real estate prices in New York City, because what he'd given her amounted to the world's teensiest thong.

A smile tugged at the corner of his mouth. "And I like those."

She flicked the sparkly fabric.

"All it needs are feathers."

Naturally, he sat up straighter. He was probably a fan of hooker heels, too. "Feathers are good."

"Men." She huffed out a sigh. Okay. If she had to do this, she'd do it right. Another quick scan of the bar promised she had time. The bartender was delivering another round to the other couple, which put at least forty feet and a five-foot bar between her and discovery.

She shimmied into the panties. Slowly. If she was showing her goods to Levi, she'd make darned sure the show was memorable. It was a curse, this need she had to be the best.

His fingers tensed on his thighs. *Gotcha.* Mr. Big Bad SEAL wasn't indifferent to her little show, after all.

The silk was a sexy tease against her skin. His eyes darkened as she inched the fabric higher, and anticipation shot through her. He couldn't touch her, couldn't come without losing their bet...but *she* could do whatever she wanted. The possibilities made her breath catch, her body tense. *Remember the* other *audience.* She shot a glance over her shoulder. Getting arrested for public indecency wouldn't help her at the DEA hearing next week. Or her job interview.

"He can't see you," Levi gritted out. "The only one with eyes on you is me."

And she liked the way he was looking at her. God, she liked it. His voice roughened to a sexy growl, his eyes darkening further as she slid the panties home. She could lean in and kiss him. Tease him some more. Dare her SEAL to do something completely wicked.

"Have you ever had sex in public before, Dixon?" His voice sounded strained.

She narrowed her eyes, barely biting back her own question. *Have you?*

"Are we teenagers? Do you want to play *never have I ever* next? Or was that an offer and you're conceding the dare?"

"No, no, and no," he rumbled. "Although I could be convinced to take back the second *no.*"

The bar had some kind of slow, sexy, do-me-now song playing on a loop. Or maybe that was the internal sound track in his head, because the world seemed to slow way down. Hell. For all he knew, he'd be seeing shooting stars or fireworks or whatever stuff women claimed to see when they were coming and wanted to dress the main event up in words. Because Mrs. Ashley Brandon rocked a thong and she definitely rocked his world.

Apparently their bet came with a few unexpected fringe benefits.

She kicked his legs apart as though the move was the most natural thing in the world, and he about burst out of his pants. He hadn't known he was capable of being shocked, but this was *Ashley*. Last time they'd discussed their feelings for each other, the words *hate* and *insufferable* had been bandied about. That latter one might be a fifty-cent word, but it summed up how Ashley felt about him. She couldn't stand him. She was supposed to tell him how he'd screwed up. Where he'd gone wrong and why never, ever on God's green earth did he stand a chance of fixing things.

Except she was standing between his legs.

And staring down at him like he was an extra-large display of chocolate-covered strawberries and she was simply deciding whether to start at the top or the bottom. And where to nibble.

He groaned.

She leaned forward, arching her back and pushing her butt up in the air. That's right, her *butt*. His thoughts got stuck on the curves visible through the folds of her dress. Man, she had a sweet ass, rounded and heart-shaped. Cup her, squeeze her—damn, he wanted to bite and lick whatever she'd let him. And hello…

She rested her hands on the arm of his chair, inching her breasts closer and closer to his face. He didn't say a word because he had no idea what he'd done to merit this VIP treatment. He hated himself for noticing, but Dixon had amazing breasts, too. It wasn't as if she'd dressed like a nun on their previous missions—he distinctly recalled a cocktail dress in a biker bar—but he'd made a point of not looking. As a team member, she'd been off-limits. *And now he was off duty, and so was she.* The cowboy singing on the sound track suddenly sounded a whole lot happier.

"You gonna ride me?" Because a dude could dream, and the way she was almost-but-not-quite touching him was fantasy material—and he wanted the real deal.

She shot him an incredulous look. Oh, boy. Someday he'd learn to keep his mouth shut, but it was an honest question. Her gaze dipped down to where—yup—he was still sporting visible signs of interest.

"You have no idea, sailor." She dropped to her knees between his spread thighs and his heart stuttered. So okay, maybe she wasn't *entirely* pissed off at him. Her long, lustrous hair spread over his jeans, her dress dipped lower, and he swore to God he felt her breath on his dick. Which was wishful thinking but…

"No touching." She flicked the hand he'd raised and he reluctantly pulled it back. Not that he had any idea where he'd planned on touching her first, but he suddenly had a list. He'd start with her creamy shoulder, nudge the strap down, and then work his way south.

"You'd like it." That was a promise he felt comfortable making. He'd make it so good for her.

Her breath hitched and then she smiled. A slow, sensuous, man-you're-gonna-get-it smile. "We don't have that kind of relationship. We're supposed to keep things professional in the field."

Which completely explained his blackmail, their sexy bet, one *faux* marriage, and the bed for two back at the villa. He'd believe things were strictly *professional* between them when pigs flew. He should probably be more concerned about abandoning the pretense at professionalism, but she eased back, giving him a perfect view of her face and chest. Her dress looked a whole lot better from this angle. It was freaking awesome. He could see straight down the front and she had cleavage he definitely needed to explore.

Except she wasn't waiting for him to get the party started. Nope. She ran her hands down her breasts like she was spreading lotion over her skin in a long, sweet stroke. She lingered when she reached the tips, cupping the heavy globes, teasing the nipples over the fabric. It was the kind of touch that got him going, had him imagining other possibilities. Possibilities like his mouth tasting her skin, his tongue exploring each delicious curve. If he'd wanted her before, it was nothing compared to how he felt now.

"If you see the bartender headed back our way, holler," she said in throaty tones and his desire for an insta-divorce evaporated on the spot.

"You give me too much credit." Right now, he didn't mind if the bartender pulled up a chair and provided color commentary.

She winked at him and damned if she didn't keep it up. She ran her hands over her full breasts, cupping and teasing, and he swore he could feel each caress.

She'd handed him a cheat sheet to her body, to what she liked, and he couldn't help but take mental notes. Softer strokes followed by harder, firmer caresses.

"That how you want me to touch you?"

She gave him another slow smile, and then her left hand headed slowly toward her flat stomach, kept right on going—he was going to have a fucking heart attack at the age of thirty-one—and stopped just above her pussy.

"I'm doing just fine without you."

"But I'm better." If she let him touch her, he'd have his hands all over her.

With a laugh, she moved to straddle his legs. Her hair fell over her shoulders as she faced away from him, the dark, silky strands bouncing out of control. The dress bunched up around her waist and her bare legs barely skimmed his, but he could feel the sweet, hot weight of her pressed against his thighs and no lap dance had ever been sweeter.

"We're touching," he whispered in her ear. When the bartender headed back toward the bar, Levi caught his eye and shook his head. Followed that more subtle gesture with the warning glare of death. *Nothing to see here.* But the guy's eyes widened slightly, probably because the man wasn't stupid and his Dixie hadn't been subtle. Jesus. He could only imagine what the man was thinking, but he probably wasn't too far off. Fortunately, she had her back to the bartender.

"And you're keeping your hands to yourself," she countered.

She danced along to the song, rolling her hips, and riding his legs. To be honest, she wasn't a good dancer. She bounced with more enthusiasm than rhythm, her butt slamming into his thighs like he was her own personal saddle and she was just learning how to ride, but she didn't hold back and *that* right there was the sexiest thing he'd seen in a long time. And when she dropped her hands to her butt and *massaged*, he lost the battle to hold back his groan.

"Having a good time, *baby*?" The grin she shot him over her shoulder lit up the entire damn bar along with certain parts of his anatomy. His blood rushed south with a resounding *hell yeah*, but he knew what she was trying to do. She wanted to make him *lose*.

It was almost cute.

"You're a dangerous woman, Dixie." He tightened his grip on the chair arms, because right now, gazing longingly at her hips, he felt like Eve faced with the apple in the Garden of Eden. One bite. One touch. Did she really have to be completely off-limits? The bet had been a stupid idea, and he could be the first to admit it. He had no idea what it would take to make her come, but damn did he want to find out.

"We'll go back to the villa."

She stilled on his lap. *Shit*. He'd said the wrong thing. Probably should have asked, not told.

"I can make you feel even better." *Please*.

Her hair slid over her bare shoulder as she examined his face. "I'll bet you can."

Making his prickly, stubbornly beautiful DEA agent come for him? No victory would be sweeter. It was crazy. This whole deal—being married, coming to Fantasy Island, letting Ashley dance around on his lap—was absolutely fucking crazy. He hadn't meant to let things go so far. He'd planned on handing her the panties and embarrassing her. That much was true. And after that…after that, well, he'd planned on letting her walk away. But then she'd touched him and he'd gone up in flames. Guess they had chemistry he'd been ignoring for a while.

Contrary to what Ashley believed, he wasn't a sailor with a lover in every port. He was actually pretty particular about who he went to bed with. Sure it had been a while, but his weeks-long stint in a foxhole didn't explain gyrating against Ashley.

Not that she'd seemed to mind.

He leaned forward and nipped her ear. "You remember the Best Ride?"

Shoot. Was he a girl? Why was he bringing up old memories when he had Ashley riding his lap?

She swung around so she was seated facing him. Kind of tucked up on his lap. "The biker bar outside Sacramento?"

"Uh-huh. That was good." And again with the Mr. Smooth comments.

She was silent so long that he figured she was pleading the Fifth. Not that he believed their first kiss had sucked. If it had, she would have told him. And then followed up her assessment with a point-by-point critique of where and how he could have improved.

"You got pretty handsy then, too," she said eventually, as if she was thinking something through. He had some thoughts of his own.

"We'll go back to the villa. Forget the stupid bet."

"Are you conceding?"

Honestly? He had no idea what he was doing other than losing himself in the moment. In Ashley.

"Does conceding get you in my arms?" Because he'd skywrite his concession if that was the case.

"I've got a penis rule you should be aware of," she said, instead of answering his question.

"Uh-huh." As long as one penis was enough for her, he could work around her rule, whatever it was. Plus he was the king of rule-breaking and they both knew it.

"Never introduce a penis to the workplace. Peens complicate matters."

"We're not working," he felt compelled to point out. A little more desperately than he would have liked.

She sighed. "But we've been coworkers and we might be again."

Her forehead rested against his shoulder. He wanted the panties off and nothing at all between them. Instead, Ashley gave him a quick, hard buss on the cheek, swung herself off his lap and stood up. Her dress fell back into place, and she looked fucking gorgeous.

She patted him on the shoulder. "Let me know when you're ready to concede, sailor."

Jesus Christ. He needed to rethink his strategy.

7

MAYBE SHE'D BEEN a little too adamant last night. She'd pushed him. Teased him. Got him all hot and bothered. But that had been the point of their game, hadn't it? So when she woke up, she half expected to find Levi in bed with her. Half expected, half hoped...and that was completely, one hundred percent messed up. She didn't even like the guy, she reminded herself. She'd left him high and dry in the bar, and he'd been every bit as turned on as she'd been.

Funny, how they'd spent the last year fighting and taking verbal potshots at each other, when maybe what they'd really needed to do was spend more time kissing. They had some serious, off-the-charts chemistry. Nonetheless, sleeping with her sometime teammate wasn't the best idea, and besides, she suspected Levi didn't know how to do anything *but* take charge in bed and she'd always avoided that kind of guy.

Regardless of how he felt about her leaving him alone with his impressive erection, he'd been back to the villa. She knew this because when she turned her head, she spotted the note next to her pillow. The paper had been

FREE Merchandise is 'in the Cards' for you!

Dear Reader,

We're giving away FREE MERCHANDISE!

Seriously, we'd like to reward you for reading this novel by giving you **FREE MERCHANDISE** worth over **$20** retail. And no purchase is necessary!

You see the Jack of Hearts sticker above? Paste that sticker in the box on the Free Merchandise Voucher inside. Return the Voucher promptly...and we'll send you valuable Free Merchandise!

Thanks again for reading one of our novels—and enjoy your Free Merchandise with our compliments!

Pam Powers

Pam Powers

P.S. Look inside to see what Free Merchandise is **"in the cards"** for you!

FREE MERCHANDISE VOUCHER

2 FREE
BOOKS
and
2 FREE
GIFTS

Please send my Free Merchandise, consisting of
2 Free Books and **2 Free Mystery Gifts.**
I understand that I am under no obligation to buy
anything, as explained on the back of this card.

150/350 HDL GKAV

Please Print

FIRST NAME

LAST NAME

ADDRESS

APT.#   CITY

STATE/PROV.   ZIP/POSTAL CODE

NO PURCHASE NECESSARY!

HB-516-FMH16

▶ Detach card and mail today. No stamp needed. ▼

© 2015 HARLEQUIN ENTERPRISES LIMITED ® and ™ are trademarks owned and used by the trademark owner and/or its licensee. Printed in the U.S.A.

READER SERVICE—Here's how it works:

BUSINESS REPLY MAIL
FIRST-CLASS MAIL   PERMIT NO. 717   BUFFALO, NY

POSTAGE WILL BE PAID BY ADDRESSEE

READER SERVICE
PO BOX 1867
BUFFALO NY 14240-9952

NO POSTAGE
NECESSARY
IF MAILED
IN THE
UNITED STATES

torn from a pad of hotel stationery and folded into an intricate origami boat. She squinted. Or maybe it was a party hat. It was actually kind of hard to tell, although she had no doubts about the sender.

Levi had been in their room again.

Read me the side of the boat nearest her declared. She tried to imagine Levi sitting there in their room writing her a note and folding it into a little paper boat, but apparently her imagination wasn't that good. When she unfolded the boat and smoothed the paper out, she bit back a smile. *If you want your panties back, meet me on the beach at seventeen-hundred hours.* No one could ever accuse Levi of being subtle.

Was she seriously thinking about participating in a panty hostage exchange? Apparently, by the way her heart was thudding wildly in her chest, that would be a yes. Or maybe it had more to do with the SEAL holding her underwear prisoner. She knew he was just having fun with her and making the best of an uncomfortable situation, but she wasn't sure exactly how far he was willing to go. And was she *really* thinking about sleeping with him?

Not that sleeping had much of anything to do with her current thoughts.

She got up and headed for the bathroom. Might as well enjoy her luxury five-star accommodations while she had them. There, she found that Levi was more insightful than she'd given him credit for, because he'd apparently anticipated her ambivalence about his invitation. He'd marooned a second paper boat by the sink on the small coconut-scented bar of hotel soap. The boat's name was the *Think About It*.

The third boat sailed across the bikini top she'd

draped over the side of the tub. She didn't even need to unfold it to read the words he'd scrawled across the paper. *Swimsuits optional*. She snorted. In his dreams.

And, yeah, naturally, he'd stuck one on the roll of toilet paper. God. What was it with men and bathroom jokes? She squinted at the small boat. Levi might be one hell of a SEAL, but he was no artist. The two stick figures were obvious, although she had her doubts about what the boy stick was doing. The rest of the drawing… yeah. No clue. Waves? Seagulls? A tsunami smashing into a coconut grove? She'd have to ask him when she saw him.

Fortunately, there was no one around to see the stupid grin she was sporting. Levi was actually kind of cute, when he wasn't trying to be annoying. And it wasn't as though she had other plans for the day. She'd check for messages from the wedding coordinator and maybe swing by the front desk. See if they had any updates from the minister or the Registry Office. Other than that…

She was a free woman with a beach date later on. She smiled every time she caught sight of Levi's origami boats, which was often enough to slow down her productivity. Still, she managed to work her way through several case reviews, and check the Google alert she'd set up about the corruption hearing.

One of the online Hollywood gossip sites had been offered photos by a party guest, and the fallout looked to be brutal. The pictures showed the agents cavorting around an expensive pool in various stages of undress. Thank God her wedding bikini pics hadn't leaked, because she would have been tarred with the same brush. She hadn't come up with any magic responses for the imaginary questions she'd posed herself from the hearing board, but she felt better prepared and that counted for something.

When she finally knocked off for the day and headed for the beach to meet Levi, he was finishing up some kind of PT routine. Muscles flexed as he dropped to the sand in a one-armed push-up before shoving upward again in one brutal move. Hooyah, indeed. Flopping onto a nearby beach bed, she settled in to enjoy the show.

Her "husband" and she might not be on speaking terms most of the time, but she wasn't blind. Levi was an impressive specimen, from the dog tags that hung from his neck to the corded muscles of his back. His shorts rode low on his hips, revealing the band of his underwear. Every inch of him was tight, rock hard and sexy, and she itched to touch him.

No touching.

He might have a pretty impressive package, but he was still the same obnoxious man he'd always been. As soon as he opened his mouth and stopped doing that *thing* with his muscles, she'd remember why she didn't want anything to do with.

Uh-huh. And pigs would fly. Levi continued to rip through his workout, and she continued to stare. Her interested gaze probably wasn't sending the right message to him at all, she realized. He'd think he'd won their bet and infiltrated her defenses, and that simply wasn't true. Last night had been a mistake on her part. She'd lost. He'd won. Today was just one more move in their silly, meaningless game.

And yet being parked on the sand next to Levi was strangely exciting. She'd never been one for downtime or playing sand lizard in the sun, but Levi was actually good company. Sure, she spent at least half her time with him wanting to groan at some particularly crass thing he'd said, but the rest of the time he was kind of fun. Not that she had any intention of telling him that. She didn't need the man getting ideas about her sexual availability or about the long-term viability of their marriage.

Rolling over on her stomach, she forced herself to stare out at the lagoon rather than the gorgeous SEAL scenery. Not that he would get ideas. She could honestly say that she was probably the *last* woman Levi would consider dating, and he'd already said he had no desire to get married. To anyone. She wasn't going to figure the man out today, so she decided to just admire the view.

The lagoon was spectacular, the water a perfect aqua she usually only saw on postcards and paint chips. She'd painted her home office almost precisely that color. Or tried to. Aegean Blue from a can wasn't quite the same as the Caribbean real deal. Just to prove the point, the sun's rays bounced off the bright blue of the water, almost blinding her as she rolled over again. Much more time out here and she'd resemble a spit-roasted chicken. A big hand dropped her sunglasses onto her face.

"Don't go blind."

The man might move like a ninja but he sounded like a ninety-year-old grandma. "Concerned, husband?" she asked before she could stop herself. She knew she sounded cranky, but Levi's perpetual good mood was starting to wear thin. Did nothing bother the man?

"I can't look out for you?" He hunkered down by her side, digging an ice bucket of miniature Coronas into the sand. Darn it. Now she felt like a heel, because while she'd been sitting her mentally bitching him out, he'd been fetching beverages. A thank-you was probably in order.

She shifted to make room for him, dropping her legs over the edge of the lounger until her toes were buried in the sun-warmed sand. It wasn't as if she had too many days with her toes dug into the sand when she was in the office, so she should enjoy. Levi settled in beside her, clearly in no rush to be anywhere. Huh. She mentally scrambled for something to say, but came up blank. They'd worked together, traded a few jokes, and swapped more insults. Other than that, she knew almost nothing about Levi.

Maybe she could have been a little nicer to him, because he stared at the lagoon, his eyes tracking a stand-up paddleboarder way out in the middle of the water. The boarder was a blonde rocking a white bikini. Despite her picture-perfect looks, her board skills sucked—she wobbled like it was a Bosu ball and she'd decided to give her core a workout. Periodically, she stabbed at the water with her paddle.

Ashley had to give the woman props. Although she'd forgone a life jacket—which wasn't her smartest move—she filled out a swimsuit well. The white bikini showcased two long tanned legs and boobs the size of personal watermelons. Exactly Levi's type.

"See something you like?" God. Please don't let her sound bitchy. Married or not, what Levi did was absolutely, positively none of her business. The possessive feeling was a revelation she could have done without. Levi wasn't hers.

He frowned. "She's not too good at that."

Um. No. But Ashley was certain the woman had other, compensatory skills. To prove Levi's point, the woman fell off the board. It was kind of satisfying to see all that perfect hair get wet. She bobbed up like a cork, too, possibly because those melons of hers weren't natural. Kind of like having your own personal built-in flotation device.

"She's determined." Ashley had to give her that. The woman pulled herself back onto the board, stood up with another marked wobble and promptly fell off again.

Levi frowned. "Yeah, but she'll be in the current soon."

The woman regained the board, stood up—and fell off. Okay. The first time had been kind of funny, but the woman was drifting closer and closer to the sea. If she wasn't at risk yet, she would be soon. A quick look around the beach showed that it was just Levi and her. No lifeguard, no concerned male companion. *Nada*. Once the woman breeched the reef, she wouldn't be getting back inside easily—and she *definitely* shouldn't be out there alone and without a life jacket.

"She's in trouble. I'm gonna go get her." Before she could respond—although she did *not* think Lieutenant Levi Brandon was remotely interested in her commentary—her SEAL shoved to his feet and headed across the sand at a dead run. His big body cutting through the air and water was a thing of beauty. Kind of like watching a machine. He pulled himself through the water swiftly with hard, sure strokes. She'd been on two missions with the SEAL team, but both had involved undercover work—and she'd been kept out of any combat. When the SEAL team had assaulted a drug dealer's compound on their last trip to Fantasy Island, she'd been left behind on the island to play bodyguard to Maddie Holmes.

Watching Levi swim was a revelation. He knifed through the water fast and hard, head down, hips low in the water as he closed the distance in a perfect crawl. When he reached the woman clinging to the paddle-board, she glued herself to his shoulders as though he was the Navy, God, and the second coming rolled into one. Ashley was too far away to hear their conversation or read the woman's lips, but a whole lot of head nodding seemed to be involved. Even from two hundred yards away, treading water, Levi radiated calm confidence. It figured he'd be good at rescuing damsels in distress. A few seconds later, he lifted the blonde onto her board and started towing her in.

As soon as he hit waist-deep water, he stood, scooping the woman up in his arms. If the paddleboarder's situation hadn't been closer to life or death than Ashley liked, she would have whipped out her camera because, hello, sexy SEAL. Muscles bunched as he lifted the woman clear from harm, water pouring off him as he made for the sand.

Grabbing their towels, Ashley sprinted toward them. The lack of a lifeguard on duty wasn't atypical for resorts, but what would have happened to the woman if she and Levi hadn't been on the beach? Maybe nothing. Maybe she would have made her way back to shore. Blondie had her head on Levi's chest and her arms linked in a death grip around his neck. A spark of something that felt irrationally like jealousy shot through Ashley. That was *her* neck. Shoving the unwanted feeling away, she dropped a towel around the woman. Blondie gave Ashley a wry look.

"One minute I was ten yards from shore. The next minute, it seems like I'm a hundred yards and headed for Cuba."

Okay, Cuba was a stretch. Outside the reef and in open ocean, however, had definitely been on the cards.

"Thank God for your husband," the woman continued with a grateful smile. "You've got a good one there. Are you newlyweds?"

"He's—" Not mine? She patted the woman's shoulder. She'd used plenty of words to describe Levi. SEAL. Determined. Arrogant. Pain in her butt. They weren't inaccurate, but she'd never thought of him as anything—anyone—more. Like *husband*.

Mine.

"He's glad he could help," Levi said, filling in the sudden silence. "Let's get you back to your villa."

COVERT OPS WERE a hell of a lot easier than rescuing hotel guests. Levi shifted the woman effortlessly to one arm, wrapping her up in the towel Ashley handed over. This wasn't his usual gig. Blow in, blow things up, blow off a little steam. The three Bs—those were his areas of expertise. But his rescuee had twined her arms around his neck in a death grip that got progressively tighter as the reality of her situation hit her. All too familiar himself with delayed reaction syndrome, he figured he could hold on to her a little longer while she got her shit together. A quick scan of the beach turned up no concerned boyfriend, husband or even another living, breathing person. Which, given how close the woman in his arms had come to wearing herself out and drowning, was probably not something he should say out loud.

Ashley tucked a second towel around the blonde

and then went to work adding a third, until the woman looked more like a mummy than anything. The layers of cotton weren't enough to disguise the case of the shakes she had, though, as exhaustion hit or the adrenaline wore off. Hell, he half expected Ashley to start patting the woman on the back and muttering platitudes. On the other hand, as long as Ashley was talking, *he* didn't have to say anything.

"You okay? Is there someone we can call?" Ashley switched into calm-and-controlled mode.

"I'm fine." The woman made put-me-down noises. "Just a little humiliated."

If he set her down now, she'd be parking her butt on the sand, so not a chance he'd let go. "No worries. Let's get you back to your villa. You got someone waiting for you?"

The blonde made a rueful face. "My husband's taking a nap. He's going to freak when he finds out what happened."

He figured the man would read his wife the riot act, followed by a lecture on basic water safety, so he didn't need to go there. Still, he gave the woman a brief smile. "Life jackets are our friends."

Ten minutes later, they had the blonde deposited on the front steps of her villa, her husband making concerned noises. Mission accomplished.

"So," Ashley said lightly as they walked away. "Rescuing fair maidens? All in a day's work for our US Navy SEAL?"

The heat crawled over his cheeks and before he could take defensive action, Ashley tugged on his arm and stared up at his face. Somewhere karma was laughing its ass off at him.

"Oh, my God. You're blushing." She sounded positively delighted, which made one of them. Before he could stop her, she whipped out her cell phone. "Smile for the camera, big guy."

"Am not." He reached for her, but she danced away, laughing.

"The guys are going to love your candids."

"I'm going to paddle your butt, Dixie." He lunged. She evaded him, but he was coming for her sure as death and taxes.

"I think that counts as workplace harassment." She feinted left and he followed. Damn, but she was quick. Fun, too. He didn't recall her being this much fun when they'd worked together before.

Wrapping an arm around her waist, he lifted her off her feet and wrestled her phone from her hand. Keeping her in place while he thumbed through her photos, looking for the picture, wasn't difficult. The woman had to weigh less than half of what he did, and a damn sight less than the last SEAL he'd deadlifted in a training exercise.

"I didn't take pictures of you last night."

She snorted. "And I didn't kill you while you slept."

He reached around and smacked her on the ass. "Don't threaten. That's not nice."

"It was just a small threat." She batted her eyelashes at him and grinned. "Put me down and give me back my phone."

"Uh-huh." He set her down, but no way he returned her phone until he'd purged it of all potential blackmail material. She'd been shockingly industrious. Not only did she have *two* shots of his bright red mug, but she had at least a dozen snaps immortalizing the GROOM written in faux diamond sparkly shit on his backside. "Checking me out?"

"Give it to me." She lunged for the camera. The move put some of his favorite parts in direct contact with a certain portion of her anatomy he had definitely *not* gotten to explore last night.

He quickly thumbed through the surprisingly small number of pictures on her phone. It was possible she didn't feel the need to photo-document every moment— or maybe she didn't have that many moments. He knew she was focused on her career and had been jonesing for a promotion. She had a cat. At least, he thought the enormous mountain of fur was an obese Siamese and not some kind of mutant mountain lion.

And bingo. Twelve butt pictures and two face pictures gone. "Say goodbye to your blackmail material."

"Destroy the evidence, but you can't make me forget." She tapped her forehead. "I've got it all stored up here. You're downright cute, sailor. It's like you've got no idea what to do when your feet are on the sand and imminent death has been averted."

"You're damned hard on a guy's ego."

She grinned at him. "Your ego's oversize. Shrinkage would be beneficial."

"You think the whole week will be like this?"

He winked at her. "Me rescuing pretty ladies? I'm willing to give you your shot."

8

GOD. LEVI WAS kind of irresistible when he cut loose. Ashley suddenly understood how he'd cut a swath through the female ranks. It would help if she could slap a Post-it note on his forehead. Something she could look at to remind herself of all the reasons getting involved with him was a bad idea. The first note would read *emotionally unavailable*. And then she'd need notes for *off-limits, commitment-phobic*, and *voted most likely to never have feelings*.

Levi was six feet two inches of hard, hot SEAL and bad boy attitude. He'd put out for every female in a hundred mile radius—except for her. Except for that one super brief, really embarrassing, scorchingly hot encounter in a very nasty alley in Sacramento, California. A moment that still featured prominently in her mental "best of" sexual highlights tape. What she needed to remember was that she was one of the boys— and the moment she slept with one of the boys, she'd move from team member to girlfriend. She'd worked too hard to risk that.

"Sun's going down," he drawled, sounding delighted.

She knew what was next. Since she didn't feel like *admitting* to defeat, she pretended acute fascination as the pathway lighting came on and the spider monkeys up in the trees started in on making a ruckus. The birds calling back and forth made decent camouflage, as well.

"So?" She'd bet he knew the precise moment the sun was scheduled to hit the horizon. That kind of information was his stock in trade. Plus the dive watch strapped to his wrist looked as if it could launch nuclear submarines.

He patted her on the back. "So, you owe me a second drink."

Rats. She'd be regretting that particular dare for the rest of her life.

She stopped walking. Might as well get it over with now, because she doubted he'd be breaking his vow of celibacy in the next thirty seconds on a very public, very uncomfortable path. What had she been thinking?

You weren't thinking at all. You were just pissed off.

She was fairly certain she'd be more careful in the future. "So what are you choosing?"

"You want to do it right here?" Levi made a show of looking around. Yeah, yeah. She got it. He thought he was in charge and the one calling the shots, which made it practically public service on her part to put him in his place.

"I'm going to win tomorrow," she informed him.

"Keep telling yourself that, babe." He didn't sound concerned. Of course when you were a big, strapping SEAL, you probably didn't have to worry all that often. She got the impression he hadn't run into too many situations that he couldn't control. She couldn't wait to turn the tables on him.

"Pick a drink or shut up." Her forfeit didn't include listening to him run his mouth. Or nicknames. "And try using my name."

"Dixon," he said cheerfully. "Nope. It's not working for me now that I've seen your panties."

He was just trying to get a rise out of her, she reminded herself. Ignore him and his new blackmail material, and he'd move on to something else.

"You strike me as more of a…" He waved a hand. "Dixie Cup."

That was not an improvement. "Sure, if you wanted to die."

"The problem with you is that you don't follow through." He tugged her along the path, his strong fingers tangled with hers. Despite the casual touch, heat zinged through her. Apparently her body was pathetic— or Levi just got her going that much. She wasn't sure which would be worse. "All these threats, and yet here I am. Completely unscathed."

"I can change that," she muttered. "Pick your drink."

"Always in such a rush, Dixie. Makes a guy wonder what else you'd be in a hurry about."

She snorted. "You go right ahead and dream, big guy."

There was a pause. Levi whistled. She tried desperately to think of a way out of their bet. Whatever he came up with, one thing was for sure. She wasn't going to like it.

"Sex on the Beach," he said at last.

"Hey. Remember the rules. No twosomes, threesomes, or more-somes. Sex on the beach is out."

His teeth flashed in the gathering darkness. "You've got two hands and ten fingers. Use your imagination."

If anyone else had said that to her, she'd be saying something catty back and probably it would be the end of her date night. Normally she hated that kind of talk, but Levi wasn't saying it to be demeaning or even because he was a guy, she was a girl, and all he could think about was sex. It was more that the man didn't have a filter. He said what he thought, and it was kind of flattering that all he could think about right now was her. Losing their bet would be impossible if he wasn't as into her as she was him.

So she let it go, let him tug her along. After a brief pit stop at their villa to collect a bottle of champagne and some towels, he laid in a course for the beach. It was dark, but not *that* dark, and they passed another couple and a housekeeping cart on their way.

"We need to wait until it's darker."

He gave her a look. "What do you think is going to happen?"

She thought about that as the beach got closer and closer. "Hotel security? Fellow guests with cell phone cameras? Bet or no bet, I'm not starring in an international incident."

Her feet hit sand. The beach stretched out before them, and it was nothing but open space, sand, and the occasional way-too-skinny palm tree. She groaned.

He smiled. "Sweetheart. I'm a US Navy SEAL. No one's catching us."

"You're a SEAL, not a ninja," she grumbled. "And I'm DEA. We usually only go where we have a warrant."

He flashed her another grin, the annoying kind that made her want to introduce her elbow to his rib cage. "I can send out invitations if you prefer."

Kill her now.

HE WAS A lucky, lucky man. Ashley strode across the sand with the determination of a SEAL team storming an enemy beach. Based on her current trajectory, she'd decided the palm trees on the far side were the most private spot in public that she could find. That, or she was just hoping to wear him down before they got there. No such luck.

Usually when he was on a beach, he moved double-time. Or carried heavy weaponry and took fire. Typically all of the above. It was strange to have the time to notice that this beach was unspeakably pretty. There were stars overhead and reflected in the water. *Jesus.* It was positively romantic and like some kind of post-card. The place even smelled pretty, much better than the last beach he'd visited. That beach had reeked of diesel fuel and other less pleasant things that happened when your beach day included six SEALs, a bay full of underwater mines and twelve surprised hostiles. He flicked the nearest palm tree with his finger. White flowers marched up the side like Mother Nature had decorated just for Dixie.

"Are we hiking to Antarctica?" Not that he wouldn't if that was where she really wanted to go, but it would be nice to know.

She didn't slow down. "You said *beach*. This is a beach. A beach without people."

He was quite aware of that. He had sand in his boots and his night vision was excellent. He grabbed a flower and followed her.

When she reached the far side, she paused, clearly assessing the trees for cover. "Is there something wrong with my choice?"

If it involved any parts of her getting naked, he thought it was a most excellent beach.

"Your beach is easy." He had to smile when she rolled her eyes. "I could put an assault team of SEALs in the water, and have them ride the surf in for the last twenty feet. A quick look for hostiles, and then we'd be up and charging all this nice, flat sand. Not too much current or chop, no underwater obstacles, plus a nice flat run in? I'd own this beach. No way you'd hold it."

She stared at him. "It's a good thing we're not dating, because that has to be the least romantic thing I've ever heard."

"We're married." Which was actually pretty convenient, now that he'd gotten over the shock of the thing. He kind of liked Ashley, when she wasn't ripping into him.

She snorted. "Don't go to my head, sailor."

"We're almost out of beach," he volunteered. Unless she decided to actually hike around the island, she needed to pick a spot, and soon.

She pointed. "There."

The patch of sand she'd chosen looked like just about every other spot on the beach, but it was lady's choice. If she said this place was better, he'd believe her. "Okay."

"Okay?" She sounded suspicious.

"Sure." It was sweet how she always wanted to be in control. Since she looked more than a little nervous, he opened the bottle and handed it to her.

"No glasses?" The lack of stemware didn't stop her from chugging the champagne.

"Be nice," he said mildly, and she lowered the bottle. When she didn't hit him with it, settling for twisting the base into the sand, he counted that as a victory.

She was nervous, he had the upper hand and somehow he still hadn't gotten it through her adorably stubborn head that all *he* wanted to do was give her pleasure. And, sure, he intended to do that by wrestling some of her famous control away from her, but she was going to enjoy it. He'd make sure of that.

She was smoking hot. Of course, she was that every day of the week, but since she'd followed him out here to give him her own personal version of *Sex on the Beach*, she looked doubly hot. Or maybe that was just him anticipating some of her clothes coming off. She wore cotton shorts that hugged her butt and a tank top with little straps. Because those straps were both thin and slippery, he'd gotten more than one peek at her bra on their walk to the beach. He knew definitively that tonight it was blue, which naturally made him wonder if her panties matched. Given how much Ashley liked things organized, he'd bet the answer was yes.

And since time was wasting, he spread their towels out on the sand and dropped down, bracing his back against a fallen palm. She eyed him, and then the bottle she'd dug into the sand. Apparently he was in a neck-and-neck race with the champagne. Before she could break his heart by opting for the drink, he reached up and tugged her down. She let him pull her back against him between his spread legs, her butt nestled up against his dick in a way that had him thinking about her underwear again. And possible ways to convince her to take it off.

It was hard to get a read on Ashley. She was a good sport, and she hated losing with a passion. So how much of her lap dance last night had been her having a good time, and how much of it had been a ploy to get him to lose their bet? He mentally replayed their kiss, too, but that only made him hard. Which she had to notice, given her current position.

Giving up on trying to figure out her motives, he plucked a flower from the side of the palm and tucked it behind her ear. "Brought you flowers."

There was a pause.

"Tell me you checked for ants first."

He stared at the back of her head. "You're worried about *me* not being romantic enough?"

She fingered the flower he'd stuck in her hair and shrugged. "So we're a good match for each other."

Were they? A good match? He kind of liked the idea of that, and it was true that they had some things in common, like being too stubborn for their own good and willing to wade into just about any fight. He liked to think he was practical, too, although Ashley kind of had him beat there. He stared at the water for a moment. Kind of peaceful, except for the nonstop hard-on he always had around Ashley these days. Sure enough, said hard-on twitched, getting bigger, and she sighed. Not a happy, soft, God-that-feels-great sigh, but a huff of exasperation.

"You might as well say it before you burst," he said.

Her teeth clicked shut. "You—"

Apparently using his erection as her backrest had rendered her almost speechless. He made a mental note of that for their future interactions, because he needed any advantage he could get.

"So I find you attractive. That's my problem, not yours. You don't worry about that."

She sighed. "Why are we doing this again?"

Truthfully, he had no idea what he was doing here.

He should let her retreat or leave or do whatever cross-eyed, stupid, incomprehensible thing it was she thought she should be doing. Problem was, he didn't know how *not* to fight. He couldn't stay down. Give up and die—or keep moving. That was how it worked in the field, and apparently relationships weren't all that different from a SEAL mission gone FUBAR.

From a civvy perspective, those missions could look…hell if he knew which word to use. Glamorous? Exciting? Purpose-driven, like that self-help shit he'd read on deployment once because it had been the only book in English. All he knew was that as a SEAL he made decisions every day that changed lives. Sometimes good, sometimes bad. Go left, run into an ambush. Turn right instead, and avoid the IED planted in the middle of the goddamned road.

He was here on this beach in the middle of nowhere because Ashley had said *yes*. That one word meant everything to him. She was funny, sarcastic, and, yeah, drop-dead gorgeous. He loved pushing her buttons and had no intention of stopping anytime soon. And when he pushed her, she pushed back. He liked that, too. He didn't stand a chance in hell of ordering her around or walking over her, and that was good. When he was around Ashley, he felt things. *Good* things. That was a nice change.

She was still talking though, and it would have been disrespectful not to listen to at least some of the words, so he tuned back in. Apparently she'd moved on from their marriage to their bet, questioning the wisdom and validity of both. Uh-huh. He knew excuses when he heard them, and she was not getting out of this. Not when he wanted it so badly.

"You lost the dare, so you gotta pay up."

She sputtered. Honestly, he figured she wasn't about to go all porno flick on him but that was kind of okay, too. This wasn't about him, but about her. He wanted her hot, sure, but he also wanted her...happy? He shoved that thought aside.

"I could help. If you let me."

She made a little noise that kind of sounded like she was choking, probably on her current situation and the out he'd just offered her. He got it. She didn't like asking for help. Didn't like needing it either. So maybe he just made sure she *took* it. Wasn't like she didn't know how to tell him to fuck off, if that was what she really wanted.

"Say *yes*, Dixie." This was a game, but he didn't want her getting hurt—and he wouldn't take the chance that he misunderstood her limits. "Give me a *yes*."

She stilled, and for a moment he thought he'd lost her. She didn't move, but she kind of shut down and he could practically hear her thinking. There were so many reasons they shouldn't do this, but the only thought filling his head right now was that she was perfect. And here. In his arms. Not touching her more was killing him, but what if he'd misread her? What if he'd—

"Yes," she said. Three letters and nothing more, but she sounded certain and that was good enough for him.

He took her down to the sand in one quick move, snaking an arm around her waist, his hand cupping the back of her head. She looked down the beach, apparently still worried about uninvited guests spotting them. He'd patrolled this particular stretch of sand more than one night when they'd been undercover on the island six months ago. He knew the security patterns, and the likelihood of anyone coming out here was low. But her worry was kind of endearing, which made him itch to tease her more.

"Let me help," he said again, then moved down her body just in case there was any question about the *how*. He figured the *why* was obvious.

He caught her legs and yanked her shorts off. Sent them flying. She'd have a bitch of a time finding them later. She made another one of those teakettle noises he was getting to know so well, because apparently he wasn't subtle enough or maybe he was moving too fast, but hallelujah, his panty guess had been dead-on right. They matched. Bright blue with teeny-tiny white stripes, the fabric was some kind of silky stuff with a peeka-boo mesh panel in the center guiding him right to his target. He definitely liked Ashley's taste in underwear.

"Are you still saying yes?"

"Yes," she sighed.

He caught her legs and dragged them over his shoulders. Her butt slipped down the towel, hitting the sand with a little bump that left her off balance. Not for long, though, because she popped right up on her elbows, still talking, talking, talking. Since gagging her wasn't an option, he needed to find some other way to shut her up. He licked her through her panties, a nice, long stroke from her bottom to the top.

She shrieked, and then slapped a hand over her mouth. See? Problem solved right there.

"This is not part of our deal, sailor." She tugged at his shoulders but, thing was, she wasn't pushing him away. She was pulling him toward her, and he could take a hint.

"I like your panties, Dixie." And that wasn't all he liked.

He licked her again, and she wriggled and gasped. The panties were kind of in the way, but they were also damned cute. Too cute to ruin since he'd really like to see them again. And they matched. Hard to find matching stuff when you only had half a set. He flicked them to one side. Her slit was pretty, kind of like getting a close-up of heaven, a dark landing strip framing wet, pink folds. Her clit was getting nice and hard for him.

"I can't believe you," she groaned, digging her heels into his back. That right there was why he hadn't backed off, because she was holding on tight to him.

"You want me to stop, you tell me." Couldn't be clearer than that. He lifted his head just in time to catch her nod. *Permission granted.*

He opened her up with his thumbs and she fell back, giving him control. He took it, too, because she was fucking gorgeous and he was a lucky man. He licked and kissed up her folds to the hard nub at the top, enjoying every second she gave him. Could have done that all night. The first minute or so she tried to hold still. She had a thing about not losing, and maybe letting him know how much she enjoyed what he was doing fell in the losing column in her book. He didn't know. Didn't care. But her body did plenty of the talking and conceding for her, coming to life beneath his mouth. She cried out, then muffled the sound. She was biting her hand, he realized when he looked up.

"Whole beach is gonna hear you," he whispered roughly, because he sure wanted to hear her. Didn't want her holding back, and *definitely* wanted all those moans she wasn't willing to share. She glared at him as if it was all his fault—which it kind of was, if he was being honest—but he slid a finger inside her and her eyes fluttered close as she gave up another moan. *So darn pretty.*

He added a second finger, searching for the right spot. Got it too, because she arched up with a greedy cry, and he covered her clit with his mouth, sucking and teasing. Her thighs trembled like there was an earthquake rocking her body, and her heels dug hard into his shoulder blades. He'd stormed hundreds of beaches, but nothing beat the adrenaline rush or the thrill of feeling her come apart in his arms. She moaned something that sounded like his name—hard to be sure since she still wouldn't let loose and scream—and then collapsed back on the sand, panting. From the blissful look painting her face, he'd done his job right.

He leaned up over her, her feet sliding down his back to rest on his ass. There were possibilities there that he needed to explore. "I need to tell you something."

"I'm not sure my brain's working yet. You might want to give it a minute or six." She stared up at him, the deliciously glazed expression in her eyes not fading, and he felt stupidly proud. He'd done that to her, made her come undone and lose all self-control. He wanted to do it again—preferably in the next hour.

"You win. I lose."

"Excuse me?" Her tongue made a slow sweep of her full bottom lip, and it was his turn to stop thinking. He didn't think she understood what he was trying to say, however. Granted he'd done most of his talking with his tongue in her sweet pussy, so more words were important. He needed to make her understand.

"We're gonna head back to our room, and we're…"

Fuck. He didn't know what word to plug in there. Have sex? Make sweet, hot love all night long? He sounded like he was quoting bad song lyrics. So he settled for, "I want you. I'm done playing games."

Reaching between them, he grabbed her hand and guided it to his dick. Her fingers curled around him and squeezed. "You're a very persuasive man, Mr. Brandon."

And she just happened to be the most beautiful woman he'd ever seen.

"Mrs. Brandon." He laid a quick kiss on her. "I'm conceding the bet."

Her fingers tightened and he almost came on the spot. "No more vow of celibacy?"

"Not a chance in hell." Only thing he wanted now was to be inside of her.

Ashley being Ashley, she'd likely make him wait for it. She liked torturing him even more than she liked winning.

A smile stretched her face. "Yes."

No victory dance, no gloating, no hesitation.

"I think you like me, sweetheart."

9

Nope. She didn't like Levi. Not one little bit.

But that other four-letter L word? Lust. Yeah, she was all over that—and him.

"You want to have sex with me? Right now?"

He smiled. Slowly. But did the bastard give her the words? Not a chance. He was going to make her do all the asking.

Fine.

She shoved to her feet, brushing the sand off her legs. Sex on the beach was every bit as uncomfortable as she'd expected—and not just because sand truly did get everywhere. She'd let Levi touch her. More than *let*—she'd encouraged him, flat-out made demands, and possibly begged. Once.

Or twice.

So she was done with the groveling portion of tonight's events. If he wanted sex, he could come to her and *he* could do the asking. It was just a matter of giving him the right incentive.

"I'm taking that as a *yes*," she told him, staring pointedly at the erection his pants did nothing to conceal.

She had him there, and they both knew it. He wanted her. After all, she might have been the one enjoying the orgasm, but *he'd* been the person doing the kissing and the licking.

God. The licking. The man had a talented tongue. She'd give him that. It was going to be hard to look him in the face the next time they worked together and not remember precisely what he'd seen and done. And since she'd already violated every basic rule of workplace conduct, she might as well get what she really wanted.

Levi Brandon naked and in her bed.

She thought about *that* while she located her clothes and dragged them back on. She could make it back to their villa in three minutes flat. Two, if she was properly motivated.

"Where are you going?" he demanded when she started toward the palm trees bordering the beach. He actually sounded surprised, which was kind of thrilling. Maybe she was the first woman to walk away from him. Maybe he'd read more into their dare than she had. But she had sand in places sand had no business being, and a perfectly fine shower that could hold an entire SEAL team if they were willing to get cozy.

She laughed.

"I want a shower," she said. "If you ask nicely, I'll let you join me."

There was dead silence behind her, but she knew better than to turn around. With a man like Levi, you didn't give him an inch. He was a sexy beast, and he knew it. Owned it. The important thing was that he didn't own her. She'd use him—and enjoy every minute of it. But when it was over she'd walk away. He'd blackmailed her into being on the island, but she'd control the rest of their relationship.

"And we need to be clear about something," she said, fisting the hem of her tank top. Navy blue cotton wasn't precisely sexpot material, but she'd work with what she had—and what she had right now was a whole lot of anger. Levi had made her forget all of her rules. Unbelievable. The man had dared her to masturbate on a public beach, and then he'd delivered one of the most mind-blowing orgasms she'd ever had. *Gratis.* He'd done so with a smile, and he'd thoroughly enjoyed himself in the process. She had no doubt of that. The Levi Brandons of this world didn't mean to leave a trail of broken hearts behind them—they just didn't realize how badly a woman could misinterpret the loving and the kissing. The touching and the sweet, sweet concern. Levi genuinely wanted her *happy.*

Damn him.

"We're going to have sex. It's going to be great. And then in the morning, we walk away from each other."

She felt him come up behind her. Good. He was getting with the program. Two more steps and she was off the beach and striding down the path toward their villa. Just in case he still wasn't on board with her plans for the remainder of their night, she yanked the tank top over her head in one smooth pull and let it sail behind her.

A big hand snapped up and snagged the fabric. *Gotcha.*

"Feeling bold?" he asked, his voice a low, sexy rumble.

Bold was one way to put it.

"You started this," she reminded him. "The beach,

the champagne, the public sex—that was all *your* idea. But, yeah, I'm not feeling shy."

His *thank God* sounded heartfelt, so he deserved a reward.

Her bra was Victoria's Secret's finest, all soft, padded curves. The satin was almost the blue of the lagoon, a bold, sexy gleam in the near dark. Black lace edge the cups, her invitation for him to draw his tongue over the soft skin. To *taste* her. Better yet, the bra had one of those front clasps, and she undid it with a quick flick of her wrist and shrugged it off.

Her SEAL didn't disappoint. He caught his breath, and then he caught her bra. See? It was win-win for him, and his curse sounded properly appreciative.

"I wouldn't want you to get bored on our walk."

"No chance of that," he muttered.

The villa was right where they'd left it—imagine that—and ten more seconds of sexual-tension-fraught walking and they were on the porch. As far as she knew, no one had spotted her striptease. And she was strangely okay with the possibility that someone else on the island had watched her walk half naked through the dark. Her body wasn't perfect, but she liked it. It had been good to her, and she planned on letting Levi reward her even more.

"Key." She motioned toward the door. He could make himself useful in more ways than one. He shook his head, but shoved her clothes under his arm and fished out the key card. It was kind of hot, the way he sort of, *almost* took orders from her. Made her wonder how far she could push him, how far he'd be willing to go.

Probably not too far, she guessed. For all his laid-back charm, Levi liked to be in charge.

He opened the door and motioned for her to go first. "Being a gentleman?"

"Not for long." There was no missing the warning in his voice. Once they got inside, all bets were off. Good. She was done waiting for Levi. Done holding back. Time to strip him down, learn that hard body of his inch by inch, and find out once and for all if he was every bit as good as she'd fantasized.

"Don't disappoint me."

He flicked her a two-fingered salute and slammed the door shut. The lock shot home, and that was all the warning she got. He scooped her off her feet, pinning her against his side as he strode for the bed. House-keeping had come by while they were out and turned down the bed. They'd added rose petals and some kind of sweet scent filled the air, which was romantic but completely unnecessary.

She didn't want romance.

She wanted sex with Levi Brandon.

"Put me down." She could walk to the bed just fine on her own, and there was nothing dignified about her current position. On the other hand, it only went to show how strong he was. She wasn't a tiny woman, and he hefted her effortlessly.

"In a minute. Consider it foreplay."

She kicked, trying to hook a leg behind his knee and bring him down. Her own special version of foreplay. Plus then she could be the one on top. He grunted and bounced her on the bed, his hands going for the waist-band of her shorts. The button popped off and disappeared into the shadows.

"Did we invite your inner caveman to come out and

play?" Her voice was more breathless than she cared to admit.

"Do you mind?" He yanked, and her shorts and panties flew across the room to join the abandoned button. She was good and naked.

"Strip," she demanded, scooting up to the top of the bed. No way she missed this show.

He shook his head but he gave her what she wanted. He sat on the edge of the bed and unlaced his boots. He had to be the only man she knew who wore shitkickers on a beach, but the sand was his problem. He grabbed his T-shirt and drew it over his head, sending it sailing to join her clothes. Perfect. Then he stood up and shoved his shorts and boxers down his legs.

Good lord, she was a lucky woman.

Naked Levi was spectacular.

Even his dick looked better naked. Not all men had a pretty penis, but Levi had been blessed in that department. His cock smacked against his flat stomach, ready to give her what she wanted. He grinned, but they both knew she liked what she saw.

"Come over here." She pointed to the spot next to her, just in case he was having any problems thinking clearly. She was, but that was Levi's fault and he could live with the consequences.

"Your wish," he said, and she just had to finish his sentence for him.

"Is my command?"

"Up to a point." He dropped down onto the bed. "I'm not into the bondage scene, if that's what you're asking."

Nice to know the man had limits.

He moved swiftly, with the reflexes of the trained SEAL he was, rolling her beneath him in a smooth

move. She made a sort of strangled noise that probably was more surprised than sexy, but then he had her
hands pinned over her head as he looked down at her.

"Are you about the bondage thing?" he asked, and
her brain stuttered to a halt. This close she could see his
eyes. God hadn't stinted when he'd made Levi. Nope.
He had gorgeous dark eyes and his eyelashes were long
and thick. He was a pretty, pretty man and right now
he was all hers.

She tugged at her wrists, but he didn't let go. Instead he got a devilish gleam in his eye that definitely
spelled trouble.

"Let's find out," he suggested, and then he covered
her mouth with his.

She met his kiss with her own, more than met him,
opening up and coaxing him in deep. Their kiss was
raw and messy, the loud kind of kiss where no one could
get close enough, but all the fun was in the trying. His
lips tasted hers, his teeth nipping and biting, the erotic
sting shooting through her body like fireworks on the
Fourth of July.

She could have kissed him for hours, her tongue
dueling with his, all tangled up with him. He tasted
like their champagne, and like something more. Something wild and wicked but all Levi. He set her on fire
that easily, and part of her resented it. When he settled
himself between her legs, she rocked up against him,
tormenting him right back. She wasn't going to be the
only one burning tonight. He was going to burn right
along with her.

He pulled back, and for once she appeared to have
kissed the smile right off of his face. Good for her—better for him. His face was flushed, his eyes blazing with

excitement, and the hard, lean planes of his handsome face were tight with need. He was right there with her.

"You're beautiful," she told him, partly to enjoy the surprised look on his face and partly because, God help her, it was true.

"You're stealing all the good lines, Dixon," he said gruffly. "But I'm glad you enjoy the view."

"You could show me something else," she suggested, and *that* put the smile back on his face.

"I could," he agreed, "but I might be in more of a sightseeing mood myself."

"I'm not a tour guide." She curled her fingers into the big hands holding hers prisoner. "Plus you've got me at a disadvantage. How am I supposed to point out the good parts if you don't let me use my hands?"

"We're gonna have to work something out," he agreed. "Or I could just go exploring."

He slid the fingers of his free hand down her body. "And you can tell me when I'm getting warmer."

She was definitely getting warmer.

If he got any warmer, he'd spontaneously combust. Dixon spread out on the bed was an awe-inspiring sight. Eyes glazed, hair all messed up, she all but screamed *I've just had the orgasm of a lifetime.* Case in point? She'd done plenty of hollering down on the beach, and since she'd made it clear that *she* believed their hooking up was a one-shot deal, he planned on making every moment count. Do it right, and maybe he could change her mind.

Once wouldn't be enough, although he didn't want to examine that too closely. Not now, when he finally had her naked and all bets were off.

Easing his hand down over her stomach, he savored the soft curve and the way the muscles jumped and fluttered where he touched her. She talked a tough game, but she wasn't as casual about sex as she pretended to be, and he liked that.

Hooyah, did he like that.

He brushed his fingertips over the faint mark from the button on her shorts before moving lower. She'd told him to find the good parts, after all, and he had ideas of his own. Her hips arched upward in sweet welcome, and he slipped a finger inside her.

Slick and sweet. Fucking magnificent.

Her breasts deserved attention, too, so he sucked a nipple in, deep. Kind of like having his cake and eating it too, because he found her clit and rubbed it. She rewarded him with that husky noise he liked so much, wiggling around to adjust the fit of his fingers. Apparently she had a few favorite spots of her own, and she wasn't shy about showing him. God, he loved how uninhibited she was. She felt really, really good, and not just the places where he was touching her.

His dick ached for her. Hell, his whole body ached for her. In the last few moments before his brain shut down entirely, turning over the reins to other parts, he recognized that he was in trouble. He couldn't think, could only feel, and while that usually wasn't a problem, this was Dixon. His occasional teammate. He had a bad feeling she was something more than an amazing lay and a good friend. He'd had good sex, hot sex, kinky sex.

She was just…more.

Probably shouldn't overthink it. He'd give her what she wanted, take what he wanted. Tit for tat. They'd get matching his-and-hers orgasms, and everybody would leave happy. His dick twitched, emphatically on board with that plan.

He switched to her other breast, loving the tight, hard bud, and her hands jerked in his. Since he only had two hands and one mouth—all currently busy—this left his Dixie free to make all the noise she wanted. Or to talk. Jesus, sometimes the woman kept up a running commentary that made him think he'd have to kiss her nonstop to get a little silence.

"Let go," she demanded, in between more of those breathy little moans. Since she was wet as hell, he was hoping those two words weren't his marching orders to leave the bed and the villa.

"You're gonna have to be more specific," he growled, lifting his head. Her nipple came out of his mouth with an audible pop, the tip cherry red. He licked it, because there was no resisting something so tempting, and she groaned.

"My hands." He was pretty sure an unspoken *you idiot* followed those two words, but he didn't feel like checking.

"Give me a good reason." Because he liked having her like this, at his mercy. Not that he planned on having much. He wanted to come, she wanted to come, and this was a damned good way to make that happen for both of them.

"Because then I can touch your dick," she snarled, blunt as always. "You're hogging all the fun for yourself."

She was complaining? He gave her nipple another lick—followed by a nip that was a tad harder than necessary. The sound that came out of her mouth was more satisfying than her words. Turned on and surprised, with a side of angry. Angry sex with Dixon would probably finish him, it'd be so amazing.

But if she wanted to touch him, he guessed he could accommodate her. Plus it would give him two hands to work with.

He let go of her, she palmed his dick and things heated up all right. He'd been a goddamn gentleman before, holding back because he didn't want to run her off.

Or wear her out.

Yeah. That was a major concern, as he had big plans for their night.

But her fingers working him changed all that. She explored and stroked, squeezing the head of his dick in a way that reminded him how badly he needed to be inside her pussy. But fuck, he guessed he was a gentleman, after all, because he was going to be all ladies first. He curled his fingers inside her, finding the perfect spot.

She was still shrieking his name—and that had to be the best sound of the night so far, knowing *she* knew exactly who'd made her come—when he slid his hand under her butt and flipped her over, lifting her onto her knees.

Before she could stop chanting his name he had a condom on and the head of his dick poised at her entrance. She was ready, he was ready, so he pushed inside her in one hard stroke. She made another, louder noise and he stilled, waiting for her to get used to him.

"Did you have to be so large?" Since she fisted the sheets and shoved her butt back, taking him deeper, that didn't sound like much of a complaint to him.

"Maybe you're small," he grunted, finding her clit

with his fingers. She squeezed down on him, so he started moving. She'd definitely tell him if he had the wrong spot. His Dixon definitely didn't hold back, so damned if he was going to, either.

So he drove inside in one hard, determined thrust as if he were storming a beach and had just the one shot to accomplish his mission. Ashley opened her mouth, probably to critique his pace, but the moan that came out shut her right up. Apparently her body liked his *pacing* just fine.

More than liked.

Because when he pulled out and drove forward again, she shoved back to meet his thrust. She was magic. Probably the black comes-with-a-dangerous-price-tag kind but she made him think of nothing but his next thrust and the pleasure consuming them both. He could feel the tension building in her, her entire being focused on the erotic friction between them. When he tugged on her clit, the rough-hard sensation pushed her over the edge.

Possibly she screamed his name—thank God for the muffling effect of the sheet—because she squeezed down hard around him. With a low curse, he pounded harder, intent on catching up. Too late for that. She'd come first, he'd come second, and she'd fucking won their erotic race.

He wasn't prepared for this. That was his first thought when his breathing slowed down some, and he could think again. She'd almost killed him, and he'd loved every moment of it. He still had her pinned beneath him, so he rolled to his side, bringing her with him. She muttered something sleepy and sated sounding.

"Me, too, babe." Bending his head, he brushed a kiss

over the top of hers. Whoa. When had tender become part of his repertoire? Unfortunately, her crazy tangled hair didn't have any answers for him, so he did it again. Just to see how he felt.

Not an aberration.

She snuggled into him, getting comfortable, and he wrapped an arm around as she drifted off. To sleep. The sex had been fantastic, but he'd known for a while now that he'd lusted after her. L word, he told himself. *Lots of L words.* His dick protested the introspection, but he had to hand it to her. Sex with her was amazing. Life-changing, make-you-think spectacular, which kind of made this her fault, right? Lust. Like. Love.

There was a really slippery slope there, one he was already rocketing down. He definitely had the lust part down, and he liked her. It was that third L word that made him feel kind of like he was drowning, but in something sweet and possibly not so scary. *Love.* He ran a hand over her arm, because he'd probably never be done touching her. She sighed and relaxed deeper into his hold.

Well, fuck. She made him feel strong. Manly. Protective.

His strong suit was blowing stuff up and leaving—and now he had to learn how to stay. He had a wife, and crazy as it sounded, he kind of didn't mind being married. If she didn't like it, she'd tell him, but for now he was going to enjoy the hell out of it.

_10_

THE RED LIGHT blinking on the room phone was innocu-
ous. After Levi had screwed all coherent thought out
of her head, she'd fallen asleep in his arms. That had
been one way out of an awkward situation. Maybe it
was the phone that had woken her up? Ashley turned
her head, not quite ready to rejoin the real world, but
the other pillow was empty.

She was still processing Levi's absence when the
man himself padded out of the bathroom, a towel
wrapped around his waist. Guess that answered the
question of where he'd gone, since his hair was wet.
And then, hooboy, she tore her eyes away from the
towel and got a good look at the rest of him. He was
hot. The towel dipped lower over his hips, leaving his
broad chest on full display, and the water droplets sliding down his skin were an invitation to touch. Weren't
they? Because her fingers were reaching for him, itching to touch the body she'd explored last night, and she
was once again turned on by Levi—deliciously, wonderfully, achingly turned on—even though she'd sup-
posedly had her fill of him.

Oblivious to her internal touch-him-don't-touch-him debate, he glanced at the phone. "We've got voice mail."

Hot sex followed by banalities was even more awkward than angry sex. Possibly Levi felt as uncomfortable as she did because he stared at the you've-got-mail light as though it held the answers to life's mysteries. In reality, the message was probably nothing more than a timeshare offer or a fifty-percent-off spa coupon. Nothing important. Nothing to worry about.

She'd had sex with Levi Brandon.

She didn't even like him. Not much. And really hot, slightly rough, absolutely orgasmic sex…that had never factored into her carefully laid-out plan for these seven days on the island. She'd broken her own no-sex rule. At some point in the not-so-distant future, it wasn't unlikely that she and Levi would have to work together again. Not that the DEA partnered up with SEAL teams on a regular basis, but they'd had some successes and she'd have to work with him. After he'd seen her naked. Seen *all* of her. Introducing sex into the workplace was never a smart move.

She stared at the light, willing it to go away. Turn off. Do *something.* Levi grabbed the phone, punched a few numbers, and listened intently. He'd rocked her world, turned it upside down, and now he was checking voice mail? She couldn't be that prosaic herself, but maybe what they'd done truly was no big deal to him. She was still trying to process that when he looked up.

"It's for us." He punched the button for speakerphone.

No kidding. Who else did he expect to be staying in their villa?

Seconds later the smooth tones of the resort's general

manager filled the room. Naturally, the guy couldn't be calling to offer them a spa discount or introduce himself. Nope. He wanted to tell them all about the hurricane that had taken a left-hand turn somewhere near Barbados and was now headed straight toward Fantasy Island, give or take a few miles. The resort had instituted a mandatory evacuation, and all guests had to be packed and in the lobby in thirty minutes.

"Guess you're stuck with me," he said, his gaze holding hers. For a moment, as she felt the intensity of his stare burn through her, she couldn't even remember why she'd wanted him gone. He seemed concerned, she'd give him that. And if *concerned* wasn't love or even affection, that wasn't his problem. He'd made his limitations perfectly clear.

"I can handle this," she said, instead of asking the questions driving her crazy. *Did last night mean anything to you? What are we doing with each other?*

It wasn't as though she herself was ready for marriage. Heck, she wasn't entirely sure she was ready for a committed relationship. Being a mature adult about Levi's priorities also landed somewhere near the bottom of her wish list. But she also wanted him by her side. Preferably with an arm slung around her waist and—just possibly—his mouth nuzzling her cheek. Her throat. She was pathetic. Last night had been too short, and she had it real bad.

Levi's eyes lingered on her face for several more moments. Maybe a few of her unwanted feelings were written there, plain as day, because he actually paused before jogging toward the door. "I'm going out," he said.

"*Mandatory evacuation* means something different

to you?" She swung out of bed and started grabbing clothes. Evacuating naked was also not on her to-do list.

He shrugged and opened the door. "I may be able to help."

Right. Because he was a highly trained SEAL and good at evacuations, rescues and managing mayhem. He could go out there and be all manly and SEAL-like, but she still wasn't going to pack his boxers and socks. And not just because he'd decided to do something that had nothing to do with her and everything with rescuing the island's guests. Those were good priorities, and ordinarily she'd have backed him one hundred percent. Only now that she'd had a taste of Levi, she wanted more. Worse, she wanted *him* to focus all of his attention on *her*. The island could sink like Atlantis for all she cared.

Crap.

"Packing's on you," she warned him in the interest of fairness.

He shrugged again, clearly not worried about his stuff. "Got it."

"I'm going to head to the lobby and confirm the evac plan." The GM's message had been detail-free, and she needed a few more data points—like estimated arrival time until the storm hit, where exactly they were being evacuated *to*, and if there were still available seats on the next flight out of Belize City.

He nodded. "I'll meet you there."

Fun, flirty Levi was gone—replaced by the single-minded SEAL on a mission. Leaving him to do what he did best, she headed out to do some self-rescuing.

Unfortunately, after she'd hotfooted it to the front desk, she discovered that getting off Fantasy Island wasn't going to be straightforward. The resort had boats lined up to take them to the mainland, but after that the destination was a local storm shelter—and not the airport. Which had shut down three hours ago. Holy shit…like this was *seriously* happening? Just her rotten luck that a tropical storm could churn up the Atlantic, hang a left, pick up steam, and be on track to cross far too close to Fantasy Island and Belize for her own personal comfort. Had karma painted a target on her butt or something?

"I thought the National Hurricane Center tracked storms." She gave the frazzled front desk clerk a hard stare. She wanted answers.

She might have grown up in the Midwest, but she wasn't completely ignorant. A full-fledged, eighty-mile-per-hour storm didn't just appear out of nowhere. Someone had to have seen this thing coming, and that someone had apparently not bothered to inform the staff of Fantasy Island—or herself—in any kind of a timely fashion.

The front desk manager smiled apologetically and more than a little wearily. "Sometimes storms change course. Now instead of a little rain, we get a Category One."

She'd just bet they did.

"There was no tropical storm watch in effect when I made my reservation." Great. She sounded like a whiney toddler. The guy probably wanted to drop-kick her into the middle of next week.

"No, madame." He shook his head. "Because the National Hurricane Center only issues them forty-eight hours in advance."

She'd carried her suitcase down to the lobby, not bothering to wait for a porter. She could do it herself, and there was no point in waiting around. She was ready to leave—but apparently she'd be doing so with every other guest on the island. The lobby was now a scene of well-organized chaos.

The manager gestured toward the line of guests filing toward the motor launches that would take them to the mainland. "Everyone's leaving. We have a mandatory evacuation."

The sky was gray and the water none too calm, but she'd seen worse. Tense anticipation filled the air as the fronds of the palm trees whipped and whistled as the wind picked up. A launch provided by the resort was small and sitting low in the water, burdened with guests and luggage. It sure beat swimming for shore, but it was also a potent reminder of why she'd gone DEA instead of Coast Guard. The only boats she liked were cruise-ship-sized, and this one would practically fit in a bathtub.

The first time she'd come to the island she'd flown in and out on the resort's seaplane. That had been more than six months ago, and plenty had changed since then.

A crewman held out his hand to help her into the launch and she kicked off her flip-flops, surveying the boat as she bent to retrieve them. The blonde from the beach shot her a wan smile, her hand wrapped securely in her husband's. They didn't look entirely unhappy though, so maybe being together was enough for them. It was a nice thought, although she couldn't imagine feeling that way herself. Which was probably why she was standing here all by her lonesome without her not-quite husband. Although in all fairness, she was certain Levi would have accompanied her if she'd asked.

And speaking of the devil…where *was* Levi? "Where are the other boats?"

The crewman shook his head, and pointed to the manager who was speeding down the dock. "This is the last boat. Everyone is aboard."

Levi was a big boy and a trained SEAL. Worrying about him was stupid, because the man could definitely take care of himself. Gut churning, she flexed her hands at her sides. Well, apparently she *was* going to worry, even though he'd probably just slipped past her and she'd missed him.

"Hold the boat."

The manager gave an audible sigh. "You can't put a hurricane on pause, madame."

"Ten minutes," she promised. "But I don't see the guy I checked in with. Contact the other boats and verify his presence for me, and I get on this boat."

She was banking on the resort's security procedures making it unlikely that they'd leave without her. Abandoning a guest on the island with an incoming storm would make their insurers itchy. Two minutes later, it was clear that Levi was not on any of the other boats. Unless he'd decided to swim for it—and even his Navy SEAL self would have been hard-pressed to make the twenty miles towing a suitcase—he was still on the island. Somewhere.

Eventually the manager—who was clearly anxious to push off and head for the mainland—finished thumbing through his checklist, and miraculously remembered that one of their guests was a security expert and had volunteered to make another sweep of the resort to make sure no one was left behind. That certainly sounded like Levi. Honorable. Protective. Pain in her butt.

She'd be happy to yell at him once she had him on the boat.

"If he was conducting a security sweep, where is he?"

The manager sputtered, eying the increasing chop of the water with understandable concern. She didn't want to get caught out in the middle of a storm either, but she couldn't just abandon Levi. She'd do the same for anyone of course. *He* wasn't special.

Right?

"Ten minutes," she repeated, clambering back onto the dock. Behind her the manager bellowed something, the wind whipping his words away. She waved a hand in his direction, and hurried down the dock.

If she were Levi, where would she go? She didn't think he was concerned about the resort's infrastructure, so he'd been checking for people. She'd start with the guest villas followed by the employee housing.

Nine minutes later, she almost ran into him. The idiot was jogging up the path. She and Levi hadn't spent all that much time together, and they'd spent even less thinking they might be married. None of which explained the sense of relief she felt when she spotted him. He was fine. He wasn't dead or dying in a ditch, although she planned on hurting him herself now that she knew he was safe.

"They're holding the boat for you." She hoped. Truth was, she didn't know how fast they could sprint a quarter mile, but one minute probably was insufficient. She turned and headed for the dock.

"I was making a last sweep. They know that." He fell in beside her and winked. "But I'm touched you care enough to come looking for me."

"It's a free world. Think what you want to think." So she didn't like the idea of him alone on the island with a storm barreling in. That just meant she was nice. It didn't mean she had a thing for Levi. "But *they* are either idiots or think you're on an earlier boat. Your ass is about to get left behind."

"Yours too, but fortunately I'm in communication with the resort manager." He waved a walkie-talkie, punched a button and then swore. "Battery's dead."

She rolled her eyes. So he hadn't been deliberately incommunicado. Just had bad equipment.

"Run faster," she told him grimly. "Or we're going to be camping."

"Got it." The rain was coming down pretty hard now, and they were both soaked. She knew he could run faster than she could, but he held back, damn him. They were three minutes past her deadline.

"You should run ahead," she told him. There was no point in being stupid about it. If anyone could hold a boat, it was her SEAL. He nodded, and took off. When she skidded onto the dock two minutes later, there was no boat.

Damn it.

She was going to have words with the resort manager when she caught up with him. Unfortunately, it looked as though first she had a date with a hurricane. Double damn.

Levi jogged back down the dock toward her. "Guess we missed the boat."

She threw up her hands and glared. "It's not funny."

Was everything a joke to him?

"Come on." He turned, grabbed her hand and started back down the dock. It had to be shock that had her following him. The rain beat down harder, making it difficult to even see the end of the dock. She wanted her money back, because this downpour looked nothing like the pictures on the resort website.

"Where are we going?" Since the airport was out, she was open to suggestions. As soon as they stepped off the dock, she sank ankle-deep into a shockingly cold puddle. Lovely.

"Dixie, we're stranded on an island with a Category One storm headed toward us. I'm not hosting a welcome party on the dock."

11

THE WIND SLAMMED into the villa and the walls shook. It felt kind of like they were camping in a kid's fort, and someone had decided to kick the blocks over.

Ashley nudged him. "Thank you."

He had no idea what she was thanking him for, so he shot her a questioning look. They were cozied up on the bed together. After checking out the other buildings on the island, he'd decided that their villa wasn't such a bad place to wait out the storm. They were in the center of the island, and there were storm shutters to pull over the windows. The public areas he'd checked out already showed signs of flooding, and at least they were dry here.

He nudged her back. "For what?"

"You want me to spell it out?" She made a face, but must have figured out that he was genuinely clueless because she laid it out for him. "You're pretty amazing in action. If I had to get stuck on a teeny-tiny island in the path of a hurricane, you're a good man to get stuck with."

Wow. He hadn't seen that coming. She liked his

body, but he knew that was a temporary thing. So they had awesome chemistry—but she hadn't admitted to anything else. And now she blindsided him with her approval? It figured. Ashley wasn't the kind of person who liked to chat about her feelings. She was tough, and she focused on the job. That was just one more reason why she'd made such a fucking amazing honorary SEAL.

"You're not too bad, either," he said gruffly. While he'd gathered supplies and storm-proofed the villa, she'd gone online and sent up a distress flare. Plenty of people now knew they were stuck on the island, so help would arrive just as soon as the wind and the waves died down some. And he was willing to bet SEAL Team Sigma wouldn't wait that long. Ashley had "accessed" the National Hurricane Center's servers too, and then backdoored her way into the systems of the reconnaissance aircraft flying into the heart of the storm. He'd pointed out that the data from those flights was close to real time, but she'd wanted "to see shit" as it unfolded. If the hurricane itself had been a piece of software, she'd have been inside it and reprogramming it to do what she wanted.

Sexy as hell.

"Sweet talker." She punched his arm lightly, and he caught her fingers in his.

The power had gone out an hour ago, taking their internet access with it, but from what Ashley had seen—and he was not asking how she'd gotten access to those servers—the storm was actually no longer on a course to broadside Fantasy Island. It would probably pass several hundred miles to the west, and they'd get one hell of a storm but not much else. The wind beat at the roof, and Ashley looked up.

They'd both agreed that candles were too much of a hazard, so even though it was only midafternoon, they were all but sitting in the dark. If shit hit the fan and conditions got worse, he'd laid out a backup plan. They'd make a run for it to the restaurant and take shelter inside the walk-in cooler. He'd considered that spot earlier, but the restaurant had a palapa roof that was undoubtedly halfway to Belize by now, plus there hadn't been enough time to empty the cooler. Spending a day or three surrounded by rotting meat and produce wasn't anyone's first choice.

On the other hand, he knew exactly *who* was his first choice.

To hell with it.

He had all the time in the world right now, so it was time to put his plan into action. He patted his pocket. He'd do this. Here she was. And here he was. He'd spent a lifetime planning like hell—then acting on instinct when he'd put the plans into motion and he was live on the battlefield. Everything in him said that he'd be a fool to let Ashley walk away from him. From *them.* What they had together was too good to let it end just because their time on the island was coming to an end.

He rolled onto his side because he needed to see her face for this. "You want to get married for real?"

"Are you crazy?" She stared at him as if he'd lost his ever-loving mind, and that wasn't the reaction he'd been going for.

"I'm serious."

"Pull the other one." She grinned at him. Clearly she didn't think he was serious, so he pulled out the little black box from his pocket. He'd ducked into the resort's jewelry store because a palm tree had already knocked the door in, and he'd figured maybe there was a back room or some kind of walk-in safe where they could take shelter. He hadn't found that, but he had found a ring. Hell, he'd even charged it to the room, leaving an IOU. He was one hundred percent, completely legit.

"Open it." He nudged her hand with the box, and she took it automatically, thumbing open the lid.

He'd liked the ring on first sight. It wasn't some big piece of bling, because that wasn't the kind of woman his Dixie was. The little sign had claimed it was a conch pearl, but he'd just seen pink. A pretty pink stone shaped kind of like a quirky jelly bean in the middle of all those flashy little diamonds. It was pretty and bold, and he kind of wanted to buy one for each finger.

She slammed the lid shut. "You can't do this."

He certainly could. He flicked the box back open.

"Marry me," he repeated.

She looked away. "No."

"That's it? Just no?" he said slowly. This was not going according to plan. He was supposed to be sliding that ring on her finger, and then he'd had high hopes for happy-engagement sex. She shoved the box at him, and he took it automatically. "You got a thing against the institution, or is it just me you have a problem with?"

"You think you're Freud now, and I should tell you all about my lousy childhood and my daddy issues?"

Whatever worked for her. The ring winked up at him, kind of a *fuck you* now that he thought about it. He snapped the box shut, and shoved it into the bed-side drawer.

"You're hot. We're stuck here." She ticked the reasons off. If she kept going, she'd run out of fingers before she ran out of steam.

"Those are reasons *not* to marry me?" He wasn't sure how he'd gone from having *I love you* on the tip of his tongue, to jonesing for a knockdown, drag-out fight, but that was Ashley and him. They were the relationship equivalent of those super-balls you got for a quarter from the machines by the grocery store's front door. They had highs and lows and plenty of bounce between the two extremes. Love her. Hate her. *Love her.*

Naturally Ashley wasn't done enumerating his shortcomings. Nope. She was just getting going, even though the wind and the rain pretty much meant she had to yell to make herself heard. Not a problem either, for her.

"You should be just a hot SEAL I want to have angry sex with. My head says *hey, fuck buddy!* But I just know my body's going to start releasing all these chemicals, and the next thing I know, I'll be bonding with you and then I'm going to be thinking about you, wanting to keep you. No, thank you."

His entire body tensed. "How's that a bad thing? I just volunteered for a lifetime deployment with you, babe. Keeping me is exactly what I want you to do."

Same way he wanted to hang on to her.

Despite the near darkness inside the villa, he could see the look of pity she shot him. "For a day, a year, forever—it doesn't matter because you, Levi Brandon, aren't keeper material."

"I don't get a say in this?" Because he really thought he should.

"You can't help what you are," she said, and then she patted his chest like he had some kind of terminal illness. "I've seen your kind before. You're darn cute, and tons of fun, but you don't know how to stick. You'll be off—first on another mission, then just somewhere else. That's the way it goes."

The hurricane meant he couldn't prove her point and slam out. Probably he should be down on his knees thanking a higher power for that rain out there, but right now he was pretty damned confused.

"So I've got a terminal case of the stupids, and you're also condemning me because you think I'm a good-looking guy? That makes no sense, Dixie. Sure, SEALs don't have the best track record when it comes to love and marriage. We're out in the field for months at a time, and that leaves you at home. But I can tell you one thing. If you're home, I'm *coming* home."

LEVI BRANDON HAD asked her to marry him. Voluntarily and without a gun to his head. Guess that made today a *when pigs fly* kind of day but she had a hard time believing he was serious. The man had a new girlfriend every other week, and yet he was waving a ring in front of her face? Whatever he was smoking, she wanted some. If she'd learned one thing growing up, it was that marriage wasn't a happiness guarantee. Exchanging vows made laundry. It made a great big to-do list, and "great" didn't mean "awesome," "really fun," or "let's do this again!" Marriage worked because the two people in it both wanted to give something to each other, and the only thing Levi seemed to want to give her was carnal pleasure. And one hell of a gorgeous ring. *Why can't we say yes?* That had to be her girl parts talking, and not her head—or her heart. He couldn't possibly be The One because she had standards—and he was a player. Levi Brandon hadn't met a woman he wouldn't sleep with. She might not settle for less than perfection, but he wouldn't settle *down*.

"Tell me why you're really mad," he said forcefully, and her tempted ignited.

"You forced me to come here. You threatened to sabotage my career if I didn't come along for the ride. Now I'm stuck on an island, and I'm about to miss my interview and blow my chance. And you want me to believe you're ready to commit and settle down with me? The only way a guy like you *sticks* is if he's hand-cuffed in place."

He winked at her, and she got even madder. Why did guys do that? "Babe, if you want to play bondage games, just ask me."

And she could guess which one of them got to play tied-up victim. "I could kill you and dump your body. Blame it on the storm."

He shrugged. "I'm too pretty to waste?"

Oh, that did it. She stomped over and rummaged in the gift basket the resort had provided. She was pretty sure she remembered a particular toy they'd included. It was childish, but she didn't care. She had a point to make.

"Don't play games with me," she snapped. *Bingo.* The resort had included a very pretty pair of bright purple handcuffs. Presumably they'd intended for her to be the one tied up, but a lesson in gender role reversal wouldn't hurt Levi.

"Jesus, Dixon." Guess she wasn't *Dixie* anymore. Good. He could keep his stupid nicknames. "I asked you to marry me. I didn't say suck my dick."

And this was reason one million and sixty-seven

why they weren't getting married. "Do you have to be so crude?"

He slouched against the pillows. For a man who'd just been turned down, he didn't look too devastated. "Do you have to walk around with that stick up your butt all the time?"

"Here's a hint," she told him, striding back toward the bed. "The next time you ask some woman to marry you? You don't follow up your proposal by telling her she's uptight and unattractive."

He opened his mouth, but she didn't want to hear anything else he had to say. Mother Nature apparently agreed with her because something toppled over outside the villa with a bone-shaking crash. When the roof didn't cave in, she decided it was probably a palm tree biting the dust. Levi leaned forward, clearly on high alert, and she took advantage of his distraction to snap the cuff around his wrist.

He jerked. Poor baby. "What the hell, Dixon?"

"I'm making a point," she said sweetly, fastening the other cuff around the bedpost before he could pull away. "You claim you know how to stick. I counter that this is the only way you'd stay put with one woman."

12

HE WAS GOING to paddle her sweet butt.

If she wanted to play kinky games, he'd do the choosing, thank you very much. He eyed the handcuff. Not that a plastic toy would stop him for long.

"Smile for the camera," she crowed, and his head snapped up just in time to meet the bright pop of Ashley's flash. That was less okay, but since he sincerely doubted she had an internet connection, he had hours if not days to scrub the picture. The storm pinning them down wouldn't be over for a while.

She paced up and down, giving him a piece of her mind. He listened for the first three minutes, but then the speech got old. He'd heard it all before from her. He was an irresponsible, pussy-loving adrenaline junkie who wouldn't recognize a good relationship if it reached up and bit him on the ass. Yeah. He'd been working on that when she'd gone crazy on him. He yanked on the cuff, but it held much to his surprise. Guess the resort hadn't skimped on its hardware. Its *purple* hardware.

He interrupted the itemized list of everything that was wrong with him. If he waited for her to finish, the sun would come out first. "You gonna at least give me a paperclip?"

"Sorry. Office Depot's closed due to a hurricane."

Had he thought he was incapable of feeling? Because he recognized the feeling flooding him right now, faster and harder than the storm water pounding through the resort. She didn't get to be the victim here, and he didn't have to be the bad guy.

To hell with it. He could break the bed, his wrist or the handcuffs.

"You attached to these?" He shook his wrist at her. If the cuffs were her extra-special Fantasy Island souvenir, he could be convinced to go for the bed.

She smirked. "You're the one who's attached."

"Watch me." He slammed the handcuff down on the bedpost forcing the lock open. Too bad all of life's little problems couldn't be solved so simply.

Ashley threw up her hands. "Is that how you fix everything? An application of brute force?"

"You talk too much." He lunged off the bed for her. She shrieked and took evasive action, but where was she gonna go? Hurricane outside. Him inside. He knew the moment she considered opening the door and abandoned the plan, because his Dixie had never, ever been stupid. Snaking an arm around her waist, he lifted her off her feet and tossed her onto the bed. Followed her down.

"You got anything to say now?" He was pissed off, his wrist ached from the he-man stunt and apparently she thought he was nothing more than a pretty face attached to a convenient set of muscles. Well, too bad for her. So he wasn't good at talking. Or feeling. Around her he was developing a whole new set of skills, even if he was still better at coming in hot and blowing his target up. Not proposing marriage to a woman who apparently didn't even like him much.

Or at all.

When his feelings had decided to come back from their vacation, they'd come back with a vengeance. Fuck if he could sort them out. It wasn't like emotions came with a preloaded label maker.

"Are you ever serious?" she hissed.

"Let's find out."

SHE'D WONDERED ONCE what Levi would be like if he ever got really, thoroughly pissed off. Staring up at his fierce face, she realized she was about to find out. He rolled, pulling her beneath him, and came down ruthlessly on top of her. He wasn't worried about giving her his weight. When her breath rushed out in a harsh gasp, he just grinned and gave her more. She didn't know if he wanted to see how much she could take, or if he had some other point to prove, but he pinned her in place without even trying.

She couldn't identify what she saw there in his eyes. He'd asked her to marry him, but that had been a joke. Or what he thought she wanted to hear. Anger? Hurt?

She didn't know, but she did have the feeling he was about to tell her. He hadn't used words like *love* and *forever*, but then, neither had she. In fact, she had pretty much cut him off the minute he'd produced that pretty pink ring of his. She sucked at relationships, she decided ruefully. She shouldn't be allowed anywhere near this man, particularly not this close, because all she could think about was getting closer. And naked.

She'd definitely take naked.

"I asked you to marry me," he growled.

Good lord, was he going to keep harping on that? She was sympathetic to the embarrassment factor, but he hadn't really meant it. They both knew that. "You've got to let it go."

He shook his head slowly. "Babe, I don't have to do anything, and you're not in a position to give orders."

Because he had her squashed into the mattress? Being bigger wasn't everything, and she opened her mouth to say so.

"Nuh-uh," he whispered roughly, lowering his mouth until it brushed hers. She shut up fast. "You don't get to tell me how I feel."

"Yet you proposed to me." She wriggled her hands free and slapped them against his chest. The man was about as moveable as a wall. If the room did cave in, all she had to do was hold this position, and she'd be fine. His hard head could take the brunt of everything, from bad weather to flying palm trees.

He braceleted both of her wrists with one hand. "Did you even think about saying yes?"

Not waiting for an answer, his mouth slanted over hers. A kiss? Not hardly. More like a brand or a mark of possession. Her SEAL felt territorial and she shouldn't have enjoyed it half as much as she did.

"No," she said, wrenching her lips from his, only half meaning it. "You popped the question, and then I popped out an answer. *You* were the one who got all pissed off."

"You didn't think I meant it," Levi said, moving his mouth from her throat to her ear. He bit the lobe none too gently and she bucked. Was that supposed to feel so good? His tongue laved the mark he must have put on her, and that felt even better. The man had her all screwed up and she resented it. "I'm gonna put words in your mouth, same way you put them in mine, except at the end you get a chance to plead innocent. You believe I'm a player, the sailor with a girl in every port."

It was true, wasn't it? "I've worked with you," she pointed out. "I've posed as your girlfriend. You're a busy man, Levi. You probably have to buy condoms in bulk. I don't think you've ever thought about settling down with one woman, and I'm not your type."

"So this makes you an expert on how I feel?" He settled himself in the cradle of her thighs.

"Make yourself at home," she muttered. The man had no limits. *And you like it.*

He gave her more weight, as if that was some kind of punishment. "Answer the question."

"Yes." She rocked up against him. Lying still like a virgin sacrifice wasn't something she was good at.

"And that's why you turned me down?"

"Pretty much." Because otherwise, on the surface of things, he kind of did look like a keeper man. He was sweet, hardworking, and as a US Navy SEAL he spent every day in bona fide hero territory. Not only did he pull a paycheck, but he made their nation stronger, safer. Maybe he fostered kittens and pulled old ladies out of burning buildings, too.

He shook his head. "And now you're stuck with me in the middle of a hurricane. Your timing sucks, Dixon. What if you hurt my feelings so badly that I pitch your pretty ass out of here, and you have to find a new hidey-hole?"

"You wouldn't do that."

"What makes you so sure?" His mouth drifted down her neck, trailing fiery kisses along her throat.

"Because you're a decent guy," she admitted. It was true. Sort of. Mostly. "Except when you're deliberately being an asshole."

It was important to be fair. And he really didn't appear to be interested in being decent *or* an asshole at the moment. Instead he gave her more kisses. More heat. She felt her lips moving feverishly beneath his, liquid heat flooding her core. Apparently the man *could* kiss the anger right out of her. If she'd planned on sticking with him, that would have been cause for concern.

He pulled back and winked at her. "Are you sure I'm nice?"

"I'm not omniscient, but I've worked with you for months. You're a US Navy SEAL and the other guys on the team trust you. So do I really think you'd stick me outside in the middle of a storm?" She smiled sweetly at him, hoping she looked more in control than she actually felt. "Not a chance. Hell, even if it was just sprinkling, there's a better chance you'd sprint to fetch me an umbrella."

"Because I'm that goddamned nice," he growled. Really? Because there had been absolutely nothing wrong or nasty about her answer.

"Pretty much." He pressed down, then up, and she sighed. Good lord, the man really did know how to turn a woman on. Maybe she should stop complaining about all the practicing he'd done. Then he stopped moving. She cracked an eye to discover why and saw a muscle in his jaw tick. He still looked thoroughly pissed, which made it all too easy to imagine him kicking down doors in some foreign country and then storming inside to clear a room of hostile insurgents. He'd get the job done. Honestly, it was sexy as hell.

Which had to explain what she said next.

"Can we stop talking and move on to having sex?"

His eyes glinted dangerously. "Babe, you really don't want to push me right now."

And see? That was their second major difference of opinion, right there.

"Why not?" she taunted. "I've got a bed, a hot SEAL and all the time in the world because I'm stranded on a deserted island. What else am I going to do?"

His hand whipped upward, her arm followed and there was a click. He'd cuffed her to the bed. Wow. Somehow she hadn't seen that one coming. She yanked her arm, but the damned thing held even after his earlier cuff-slamming act.

He gave her a tight smile. "I didn't break it, Dixie. Just forced it open. The lock still works."

Crap. She bucked, but he was already sliding off her. He reached for the utility knife on the bedside table. "Useful," he observed and the blade flashed before she could even catch her breath. Cold metal slid down her chest and over her stomach.

"Don't you dare—" Red flag to a bull. The blade sliced through fabric.

"Don't *what*?" Oh, Mr. Big Bad SEAL didn't like *that*. Boo-fucking-hoo. Her clothes were probably sitting on the tarmac at Belize International Airport, and he'd just destroyed her last outfit. If anyone got to be pissed here, it was her. Not done with her yet—thank God—he pulled her shirt and bra open. The knife disappeared, tossed somewhere, and he yanked down her shorts and panties. She went up in flames, anticipation flooding her. The storm pounded outside, and all the anger and fear and adrenaline needed some place to go. Why not take it out on Levi?

"Don't stop." She slapped her free hand around his erection. "You volunteered to make this mine, so consider this a trial run."

"You said no," he growled.

Semantics. But he rolled off the bed and jerked his shirt over his head. Five seconds later his pants hit the floor.

"Condom," she demanded.

"Absolutely." They both knew he was clean, because he'd just had a physical and she didn't doubt he was careful. He rolled on a condom, fisting himself in a vise that looked tight enough to hurt, but he groaned, and damned if that didn't sound like a happy noise.

"And now I'm saying yes," she snarled. "So hurry up."

He lifted her hips, kneeing her thighs apart. She rocked back, wrapping her legs around his hips. No way she was letting him take her. She'd be getting her own piece of him, making him hers for the moment. He eased back, then drove forward, and she lost her breath. There was nothing gentle or easy about Levi. He slammed himself home, pushing deep until his hips were sealed against her pussy, and they were both breathing hard, like they'd just run a race and were headed neck and neck for the finish line. He didn't beat her. Not now, not today.

"Is that all you've got?" she taunted him.

"Not. Even." He pulled back, thrust again and each brutal drive shoved her higher, further. He was rough but oh, God, the pleasure was right there along with the burn, and she'd never felt this alive before. The wind howled outside, the villa shook and she wanted more—more Levi, more inside her to fill up the empty place she hadn't realized she had. She needed him, and he delivered.

"Don't stop." Shoot. That came out more whimper than demand.

He curled the fingers of one hand around hers. The other cupped her butt, lifting her for his next thrust. She was spread wide-open, legs cradling his hips. Each thrust drove her into the mattress and it felt so fucking good. The raw burn of him branded her from the inside out as he pounded his way home. This was what she'd needed, what she'd craved. When she came it was rough and hard, her body clenching down on his, holding on and not letting go. This was powerful on a whole new level, and when he followed her over the edge, with her each step of the way, it was pretty damn perfect.

13

DIXIE FELL ASLEEP after sex. Uncuffing her from the bed, he pressed a quick kiss against her wrists and tucked her against his chest, making a mental note to tease her about the falling-asleep thing later. Couldn't have too much blackmail material when you had a woman like that in your life. *Temporarily*, he reminded himself. As soon as the storm passed and Belize got its act together, they'd get divorced or annulled or however folks stamped an expiration date on marriages down here. He didn't get to keep her.

About an hour later, the wind died down. Since he was itching to take a look, he got out of bed, pulled on his boots and headed for the door. There might be more storm coming, but he'd be quick. The paths around the bungalow were inches deep in water, and it looked as though half a jungle had been spread over the concrete surfaces. He debated moving up to the lobby, but their roof looked good, and the bungalow's position would likely protect it from the worst of the wind.

Ashley padded out behind him. He told himself her

coming out here wasn't a good thing. He needed her inside where it was safer.

He turned his head and looked at her. "You're gonna get wet."

Undeterred, she slid arms around his waist. "Nothing sweet about me. I won't melt."

Something in his chest lurched. Sank toward his stomach or his knees. He had a bad feeling it might have been the heart he didn't think he possessed. His Dixie was plenty sweet despite her tough-girl exterior.

"Not true," he said gruffly, ignoring her muffled snort of disagreement. Didn't matter what she thought—just how he felt.

"Storm's not over yet," she said finally, backing away from their moment.

She wasn't wrong—he could feel the wind picking up, the rain beating down on their palm tree canopy with renewed strength. Safest spot now was inside. He swung her up and dropped her over his shoulder.

"Hey!" She swatted at his butt.

"Don't teach me your kinky habits, Dixie." He strode back inside, pausing just long enough to secure the door before he dropped her on the bed. She stared at him a moment, then laughed.

"You're incorrigible, aren't you?"

"Secret's out." He scrounged up a towel, because her feet had gotten wet chasing him outside and that was another thing he could fix. She let him, which was as gratifying as it was surprising, although when he'd finished, she grabbed the towel from him and ran it over his arms.

He watched her for the next few minutes as the storm roared over them with renewed vengeance. She was nervous. She hid it well, but with each crash of the wind against their bungalow, she jumped. Since he couldn't promise it would all be over soon, he rummaged in the gift basket for a distraction. Even he wasn't ready to tackle the Purple Monster, but Truth or Dare? Yeah. That might work. Returning to the bed, he set the flashlight he'd retrieved from his bag down in the center.

He flicked her on the nose. "Budge over."

"You want to play board games?" She eyed the little box in his hand. She'd pulled on his T-shirt for her porch reconnaissance, but otherwise she was naked. Ordinarily, he wouldn't have complained about nudity—hell, he was all for it—but if they had to evac, clothes would be preferable to no clothes. On the other hand, he had a go bag ready by the side of the bed, and so far the worst of the storm appeared to be avoiding Fantasy Island. Maybe he could take a chance.

He tossed the box at her. "This isn't just any game. It's a test."

She caught the box and promptly dropped it on the bed. "Not interested."

"You'll like it." He was sure of that.

Of course, his Dixie had to be the world's toughest audience. "Convince me," she ordered.

"You get to make me spill all of my deepest, darkest secrets." He turned the flashlight on the box so she could read the label. "You're a female. Aren't you supposed to be into that?"

She snorted. "I thought you were an open book. Have you been holding out on me?"

He grinned at her. "Only one way to find out."

A particularly strong gust of wind pounded on their roof and she jumped visibly. Yeah. He needed to fix that. Scooping an arm around her waist, he pulled her back between his legs and wrapped his arms around her. She made a soft sound and relaxed into him. *One problem solved.*

"I'll even let you go first because I'm such a gentleman."

"Uh-huh." She didn't sound convinced, but she opened the box and thumbed through the cards.

"I'm not sure you're supposed to read them first." He'd admit that he didn't know the rules to Truth or Dare: The Married Version.

"Quality assurance check, Brandon." She grinned and plucked a card out of the very back. "Truth. Do I act more like your mom or your dad? Oooh. Freudian."

Okay. So a game wasn't his best idea. The Purple Monster looked more and more user friendly by the second.

"Maybe we should start with *dare*." He reached around her and grabbed a card. "See? This one challenges me to act as your sex slave for the next fifteen minutes. That one would be way more fun."

She lifted a shoulder. "I'm more interested in hearing an answer. You picked the game, so don't bitch if you don't like the question."

"Gotcha." He wrapped his arms more tightly around her waist and blew in her ear. As though he didn't mind in the slightest if she poked every sore spot in his psyche. "Mom."

"Ewww. Really?"

"You want me to compare you to my dad? He was Marine Corps tough to the end, and he didn't have a good-looking bone in his body."

"Not a SEAL?"

"Nope. I was a disappointment to my old man." Joining the Navy had been one more way to flip his dad off. Give the man almost what he wanted—but not quite. Levi had been lucky that the Navy turned out to be the perfect fit for him.

"What was he like? I don't even know where you're from." Her brow got that adorable little crinkle again, like he was a puzzle she needed to solve. He ran a finger over the crease.

"I'm from San Diego. You know that."

She gave an exaggerated sigh. "That's where you're based. Where did you grow up?"

"Here, there and everywhere. My dad was a master sergeant and we moved from post to post every eighteen months."

There'd been plenty of families like his. You lived in base housing, went to base school with the other kids. He'd climbed on more tanks as a boy than he had jungle gyms. On the upside, he'd gotten to fire an M16 when he was eight and that had to be every little boy's dream come true. And the moving about hadn't been so hard. Sure, he realized now that there hadn't been a whole lot of money, although none of them had ever gone hungry even if there had also been plenty of days when his mom threatened to put a brick on his head to stop him growing out of his clothes.

"Was it hard?" She sounded genuinely curious, so why not tell her?

"Like trying to live your life on a plane bucking in the wake of a fighter plane," he admitted. "The new place and new school wasn't so bad, but my mom had to hold everything together. She was a strong woman, but she and my dad fought. He'd leave for missions, and we'd be left behind again. My mom wasn't a fan of his missing every milestone, picnic, and play." He stopped, not entirely sure why he was telling her this. Her fingers stroked the back of his hand and for a moment he just let himself enjoy. "Pictures couldn't make up for what he'd missed. He was a good man and I respected the hell out of him, but it's hard to be close to someone who's never there, no matter how good the reasons. Some people made it work. Others got divorced, had affairs, or fought like they were auditioning for a reality TV show."

Ashley got a funny look on her face, as though she didn't know if she should console him or laugh. Yeah. He'd felt like that too many times himself. So it was time for another distraction. He plucked a card from the box.

"My turn," he announced. And wouldn't you know… he'd pulled a dare card. He read it and grinned. "I'm supposed to provide oral satisfaction for three full songs. Any chance you've got the 1812 Overture on your phone?"

She smacked him, but then she let him kiss her, and before long the storm overhead was just the best kind of background music.

"STORM'S PASSED, DIXIE," Levi pressed his mouth against her ear causing delicious goose bumps in all sorts of places, and she debated pretending she hadn't heard him. She wasn't quite ready to end their stranded-on-a-desert-island adventure. But that was thing about reality—it insisted on intruding. Levi had commitments, and so did she. She couldn't hide in bed with him all day, no matter how much fun it was. Part of her wished she could coax him to stay, but that was another all-too-real fact. Levi wasn't the kind of guy who stuck. He rode in on his white horse—or on a Sikorsky UH-60 Black Hawk—he fixed the problem and he left. He was good at his job, and she was certain he could prove his worth in a number of ways, starting with her lack of a decent sex life. But there was no denying that his first loyalty was to SEAL Team Sigma, or that he'd be heading back to base and back out into the field long before she was ready to be done with a relationship.

With him.

Outside the bungalow, things were quiet. The rain had finally petered out, and the wind had stopped trying to tear the roof off their hideaway. Bright sunlight filtered through the windows—Levi must have rolled back the storm shutters at some point because she could clearly hear the sound of waves crashing on the not-too-distant beach. The waves would be high, fueled by the storm. A good day for surfing.

Levi's proposal last night had been awkward, and she didn't know what to say now. He'd asked her to marry him—for real this time—and she'd refused. Then they'd had angry sex, followed by something else. Something she had no words or labels for, although she knew something good when it took her to bed. Finding out they might be married had been a huge shock, so she wasn't sure why or how the *will you marry me* words had ever left his mouth. But she figured he'd been trying to look out for her, to give her what he thought she needed.

At least once an hour he got that slightly panicked look in his eye that told her he was wondering what the hell he was doing. Here. Or with her. And then he'd get up and start moving, as though a little hard-core exercise or a change in scenery could fix his itchy feet. Thing was, she had the same doubts. Somehow they'd moved from being frenemies—at best—to being friends with benefits to…this. She didn't need him to give her a ring or flowery words. She just needed a little more of him, a few more minutes in his arms. Then she'd be able to get up and go back to her life, and he could stop panicking quietly.

Levi nuzzled her neck, skimming his mouth over the sensitive skin there. She loved the way his five-o'clock shadow teased her skin, just a hint of the rough and tough man lurking beneath Levi's surface. She liked that his arms were hard and that when he held her, he held her just a little too tightly and a little too close. All of that meant that the sound of a helicopter approaching overhead wasn't entirely welcome. She listened for a moment to the steady beat of the blades and wash of sound as the bird banked over the island and came about.

"Sounds like the cavalry's here."

"Uh-huh." Levi didn't sound like he was in any hurry to leap out of bed and flag down their potential rescuers. Was she supposed to leap up? To stay? And if she did, what then?

"Hey." Levi nudged her, dropping a kiss on her nose. "Stop thinking so hard." He tapped the crinkle on her forehead.

One of them had to think. They both needed to get up, get dressed and go meet whoever had just landed on the island. She needed to get back to the mainland and catch a flight to Virginia. If she was lucky, there'd be a commercial flight sometime in the next few days, and she might actually make her hearing on time.

Someone banged on the door. Hard.

Levi swung his feet over the side of the bed.

14

IT HAD BEEN all of thirty seconds since she'd had her hands on his large, toasty body, but she felt the loss keenly. Answering the door suddenly seemed a whole lot less important than dragging Levi back to bed and having her wicked way with him.

"Levi—"

"What?" He grabbed his pants and yanked them on without breaking his stride. She had no idea what she'd intended to say, and then the moment was lost entirely when Levi flung the door open mid-knock. An entire crowd of people stood on the bungalow's porch, all peering inside their room like they were some kind of zoo exhibit. While looking at Levi's half-naked body was still fun, the sexy factor now hovered somewhere around zero. She'd gotten her sex-in-public fantasy out of her system on the beach with Levi and had moved on.

"Nothing," she said finally, although maybe he'd been talking to the assembled horde and not her, because various people all started talking at once. *Didn't realize you'd been left behind, grievous oversight, so glad you're fine.* Blah-fucking-blah. She wanted another day alone with Levi. An hour. Even five minutes. Not that she had any idea what she would have said to the man, but she was certain their time would have involved kissing. Among other things.

He leaned against the doorframe, and she wanted to leap out of bed and lick him from head to foot. His sweatpants hung low on his hips and he was barefoot. He was also rumpled, cut, and no longer hers. He turned his attention to their visitors. His wide shoulders blocked her view, but she counted at least five pairs of legs sticking out beneath rain ponchos. Two wore BDUs and steel-toed boots, which made her guess Belizean military. Two pairs of cargo pants. And one suit with a very nice pair of wingtip shoes. Unfortunately, her inner hussy wasn't interested in the sartorial details of their rescue party. *Slam the door. Come back to me.*

Levi apparently didn't share her interest. He didn't act surprised to see their company, either. Or disappointed, reluctant, or otherwise unhappy. She definitely wanted to hold that against him.

"What's the plan?" Okay. So he was also more focused on leaving than on her. The weather hadn't entirely cleared up and rain gusted inside, painting him with tiny droplets.

The guy in the suit turned out to the resort's general manager, who had immediately commandeered the first available helicopter to fly out to the island and rescue them. Ordinarily, she would have applauded his efficiency. He was handling the logistics of getting them both off the island with speed and discretion, so now probably wasn't the time to ask for late checkout.

She got out of bed and padded over to the door. The manager ran through the new evac plan with smooth efficiency, Levi nodding along to each point. The *comp your stay, of course* part was good news, but it appeared they'd be riding out of here one at a time due to limited capacity in the chopper. Whatever. She waited for Levi to protest, but he didn't say anything.

The manager hesitated. "One more thing."

"Shoot," Levi said. He was back in Navy SEAL mode. She could practically hear the gears whirring in his head as he assessed the evac options and came to conclusions. Without consulting her, she reminded herself. She appeared to be playing best supporting actress in this script, or maybe she was just the scenery.

"We've just heard back from the Registry Office. They have no record of your marriage." The manager kept his eyes discreetly pinned on Levi's face. It was like she was wearing an invisibility cloak. Or maybe the manager wasn't comfortable with the fact that she was wearing just Levi's T-shirt. It had to be obvious what they'd been up to.

She looked at Levi.

Levi looked back at her.

The man could make a killing at cards because he had a poker face nobody could read. Hooboy. But the wedding update was good news and better news. Wasn't it?

"So since you didn't sign an application and the license was for a different couple, resort management believes it's safe to say you're not married."

Levi gave her another inscrutable look that she decided to interpret as *Let the celebrating commence.* This was what she wanted, she told herself. What they *both* wanted. She had a great job, a shot at an even better promotion, and a generally all-around awesome life. Adding a husband to the mix would be stupid. She didn't *need* a husband. She didn't even want one. Did she? Since she didn't want him to think she felt anything other than relief, she tugged him away and tossed him a conversational softball as she slammed the door on Fantasy Island's management team.

"You're rescued."

"Excuse me?" He slid her yet another look she couldn't interpret. Maybe she should blindfold him in the interests of making him easier to understand. Just in case her two-word explanation had been that difficult to parse, however, she rephrased.

"You're still a bachelor. Not married in the slightest. Free to go about your business."

She gestured toward the door she'd slammed shut to emphasize her point and get him moving, but he just stared. Apparently they were not on the same wavelength. Frankly, she had to wonder if they were even speaking the same language. They couldn't part ways too soon, and she needed to tell him that. Just in case, you know, he thought she'd miss him.

"And by the way?" She strolled back toward the bed. She'd definitely miss the mattress. It had been awesome.

"What the fuck do you want now?" he growled. Really? That was his idea of an answer? As far as husbands went, he sucked. If he ever planned on getting married for real, he should take communication classes. Read a self-help book. Grovel. Since she wasn't poor, future Mrs. Brandon, she didn't particularly care, but the man needed serious work.

"You didn't win our dare," she reminded him, making her tone deliberately sweet as she stretched out against the pillows. The way his eyes flared, his mouth

was getting rescued, she'd do it with minty fresh breath.
Had they even used a condom last night? What if it
broke? What if they *had* been married? Then they'd
have fucked up

snapping shut, was satisfying. Really, really satisfying. He'd had sex. He lost. See? Everything was black-and-white again. "Your ass has been officially voted off the island."

"Are you serious?" He dropped down beside the bed, his hands slapping down on the mattress beside her. The surprise on his face was kind of endearing, as if her little announcement had actually blindsided him. "You're holding to the terms of our *bet*?"

Um, yeah. Of course. She should have known he'd question her. When had Levi ever done anything she asked without challenging her? The man asked a million pointed questions, all intended to undermine her authority and whatever it was she was doing. If he ever agreed with her, she'd probably drop dead of shock.

She was tired—because someone had kept her up all night having sex. She was also pleasantly sore, close to ravenous, and unexpectedly cranky. He'd been a considerate lover, making sure she'd come. It was so freaking perfect it was unnerving. For not the first time she understood why he had women lining up to date him. No. Wait. *Date* wasn't the right word. Why couldn't he just be the total jerk she'd believed him to be? Why did he actually have to be nice? Booting him off the island was the only option she had, because otherwise she might be tempted to go for a second night. And absolutely nothing could come of that.

"You lost the dare," she repeated with a tiny wobble in her voice. "I won. That means you leave the island. Do not pass Go. Do not collect two hundred dollars. Immediately leave the island and stay the hell out of my life."

"That's it? We have sex, and you show me to the

door?" He didn't look so *nice* now. Nope. Her SEAL looked pissed off.

"Seriously, were you expecting wedding bells to ring for real?"

She knew he was a player. Accepted it. Sure he hadn't said as much, but she knew how guys like him worked. They charmed the panties off a girl and then they bugged out the morning after. It didn't matter if she'd like to believe Levi felt differently about her and that his marriage proposal had been more than a random impulse due to their forced proximity. The only feelings he'd mentioned last night had been the familiar L word feelings—lust, lust, and more lust. And that had been what she wanted too. Coming out on top in their dare had been an unexpected bonus.

His jaw tightened. "Was this all a game to you?"

"I *thought* I was being blackmailed. If I'd known tropical island attendance was actually optional and not mandatory to prevent the release of certain incriminating photos at an ill-timed juncture in my career, I would have stayed in Virginia," she pointed out. "I *thought* there was a good chance we were married. I *thought* I'd deal with the problem."

"You weren't *thinking* last night," he cut in.

"No." He had her there.

"Did you have sex with me just to win a dare?" He sounded incredulous.

She gave him the once-over. Yep. He was just as gorgeous as he'd been the night before. "I don't think so."

"How can you not know?" He was half-naked and rain-kissed from his trip to their front door. Too bad the no-sex rule was back in force, because she had an itch to trace one particular water drop that was inch-

ing its way past his dog tags and down his very sexy, very cut chest.

"Oh, come on. You didn't want to really be married."

He looked at her and she felt her cheeks start to burn.

Returning to bed had been stupid, and it gave him the advantage.

"Move," she ordered, swinging her legs over the side. She spied her panties halfway across the room. Normally she'd…she had no idea what she'd normally do, because there was nothing *normal* about this. She stood up. He could either fall back or get stepped on. His choice.

"Jesus, Dixon. Don't have a heart attack." Naturally he didn't move. God forbid *he* made the first move or offered a concession. She knew she wasn't being entirely reasonable, but when she looked at him, an unwelcome little voice in her head started up a whole chorus of what-ifs. *What if Levi stayed? What if they actually tried to work out their relationship? What if last night had been* more *than just sex?* She brushed past him and headed for the bathroom. He stood up and followed her.

Naturally.

"I'm using the bathroom," she snapped, grabbing the robe the hotel had provided. "Get out."

Naturally, he followed her. The man couldn't take a hint if it was tattooed on his mighty fine butt.

"I think we need to talk." He closed the door—shutting them both in the bathroom. That was not what she'd had in mind, and she opened her mouth to tell him so. "This is my room, too."

Now he got territorial on her?

She dumped the contents of her toiletry bag out onto the counter, rooting around for her toothbrush. If she erally. Squirting toothpaste onto the brush, she glared at him in the mirror.

"Out," she snapped. "O.U.T. It's pretty damn close to I.O.U., which is what you do."

His NOT-WIFE jammed her toothbrush into her mouth and started brushing hard enough to scrape the enamel straight off her teeth. Apparently the hurricane hadn't dented her plans for oral hygiene. Maybe she had a dentist in her family tree.

"You're holding me to our bet?"

She rinsed her mouth from a bottle of water, spat and pointed the toothbrush at him as though it was a semi-automatic. "You held me to it. *Twice.*"

"You enjoyed it, too. You give an amazing lap dance." He grinned, which was a mistake, because the toothbrush came flying toward his head. He caught it. Good thing it hadn't been the water bottle, because right now he'd had enough water to last him a lifetime.

"You had sex. You lose."

"It wasn't that bad," he said, and the situation in the bathroom shot to Code Red.

"You came. I rocked your world." She narrowed her eyes.

"Could have been faking," he suggested, and she snorted.

"Give the man the Oscar. Did you even consider the possibility that you would lose?" She held out her hand for the toothbrush. He considered hanging on to it—

maybe Ashley would try to retrieve it herself?—but then gave in and tossed it to her.

"Not really," he admitted. He'd been trained to win at all costs. Not having sex for a week hadn't seemed particularly challenging, although he clearly hadn't factored in the effect that Ashley had on him. Plus they'd been married, or so he'd thought. Married people had sex. It wasn't a big deal.

Ashley didn't look sympathetic, though. "So think about it now. While you pack."

Grabbing a towel from the rack, he rubbed it over his damp chest. "You really want to get rid of me that badly?"

She froze. "Geez, Brandon. Put your clothes on."

"Why?" He shrugged. "You've already seen everything I've got."

"I don't need to see it again," she snapped, but he noticed she didn't look away from the mirror. He was pretty sure she could see every inch of him, which he decided was encouraging.

Since he definitely liked the idea of her looking, he took twice as long as he needed with the towel. She finished brushing her teeth, and moved on to doing something to her face with some kind of white cream. Since she'd gone back to ignoring him, he moved behind her and snagged the jar when she set it down. Wrinkle cream. He examined Ashley's face.

"You need this stuff?" Because the only line he saw was the pissed-off pucker she got between her eyebrows. Usually when she was talking to him. Or thinking about him, spending time with him or just standing in his general vicinity. Come to think about it, the only time he hadn't seen that line was when they'd been in bed, which was reason 1,213,457 for getting between the sheets together again. "It's just gonna wash off as soon as we step outside."

She snatched the jar back and growled, "Towel."

He looked down at his bare chest. Okay. So he'd gotten a little wet. Was this an expression of wifely concern? *Not your wife,* he reminded himself. Which was a good thing. He couldn't do married, and failure was unacceptable.

"You sure you want to get rid of me?"

She gave him a look and slapped a second towel into his arms. "You have no idea."

"So tell me what you're thinking."

She leaned back against the sink and crossed her arms over her chest. The robe gaped and he dragged his gaze back up. Her face screamed sex, too. Her long, dark hair tumbled everywhere, messed up from his fingers, and her lips were pink and kiss-swollen. He could see the red marks from his beard on her throat, and he'd bet she had some lower, too. If only he could convince her to lose the robe. He liked looking at her. Liked seeing her wearing his mark. It was sexy. Perfect.

Not his usual thing.

"We're not married," she said. "So everything's easier. Getting a divorce could have been difficult to explain."

Which was just one more way they were different. Even if they had turned out to be married, it wouldn't have been the end of the world. She was much more worried about what other people thought—and about how *she* thought he lived his personal life. Would he really be such a bad husband? Part of him kind of wanted a shot at showing her how good he could be.

Wait. Did he really want that?

He did fun, casual sex and he didn't want a wife. She didn't want a husband. Apparently some previously undiscovered part of him didn't care about those wants, because *it* wanted to hang on to Ashley. Real tight. *She's not ours, you idiot.*

"You have to leave," she said fiercely.

"Whatever you want, babe." If she wanted him to go, he'd go.

15

THE RIVERBOAT CASINO was rocking. Levi had dropped mortar that was quieter. Still, hundreds of gamblers, drinkers and partiers made happier noise than hundreds of 81 mm rounds pounding into an Iraqi palace. He'd spent that particular desert "party" taking the rounds closer and closer to the group of insurgents holed up behind the walls and laying down enough fire to keep the SEAL team from advancing. The riverboat wasn't a bad change, and he'd been happy enough to come out here when he'd gotten the invite to the joint bachelor party for Mason Black and Gray Jackson.

Too bad his heart felt so damned heavy.

Sometime between when he'd swung by Quantico and blackmailed Dixie into joining him on a Belizean adventure and when he'd hightailed it back to the mainland, that organ had taken a direct hit. The SEALs had commandeered a booth in the front of the bar that fronted the casino floor because *we're always on the frontlines* or so Gray claimed. Their seats gave them an excellent view of the casino's goings-on, although most of the guys were more interested in giving Gray and Mason a hard time about their upcoming weddings than in checking out what was happening on the floor.

What was Ashley up to? Had she scored her promotion? He knew she'd knocked them dead at the corruption hearing, because he'd watched the videos on C-SPAN. She'd fielded every question lobbed at her like a pro, giving her testimony about what she knew to be the truth as unflinchingly as any SEAL leading a run under enemy fire.

Work hard. Play hard. That had been SEAL Team Sigma's informal motto for the years they'd fought together. The upcoming weddings were good things, but Levi had to wonder if the team would change afterward. Mason and Gray would be more than just SEALs. The *lover* label wasn't the challenge, but *husband* and, way down the road of the future, maybe *daddy*? Yeah. That was weird. But his brothers seemed to welcome the new claims on their loyalties and hearts. Fuck. He'd never imagined the day would come when he'd be thinking about *hearts* as anything other than a target for his M4, but things changed. *He* changed.

Not that he seemed to get credit for changing. As far as he could tell, he still fell into the category of The Last Man on Earth in Ashley's romantic universe. She didn't want anything to do with him—enough so that she'd kicked his sorry ass off her island. He really needed to stop betting, at least on things that mattered. Standing up, he grabbed his untouched beer and made his escape from the table.

The bar was on the second floor, and he had a bird's-eye view of the casino floor below. The machines buzzed and whirred, generating a crapton of noise as people won and lost. He should go toss a handful of quarters into the slots, and raise a beer to celebrate his friends' luck in landing two very special ladies. The casino floor—and Louisiana—was the last place he wanted to be, however.

A shoulder bumped his and he looked up. Figured that Mason had sneaked out of his own bachelor party. The poor besotted guy appeared to be counting the days until he slid a ring onto his bride's finger. Right now, though, he looked concerned, which officially made Levi the Party Loser because apparently Mason had come out here to make sure *he* was all right.

Mason leaned against the railing. "You want to talk about something?"

Not really. "Did proposing turn you into a girl?"

Mason grunted something. Probably safe to assume it was a negative. There was a beat, and then he asked, "You didn't really marry Ashley, did you?"

Apparently the word hadn't gotten around yet.

"Nope." He saluted the other SEAL with his beer. "We still don't know how our names ended up on the certificate, but there's no license and no record of a wedding."

"So you're still single."

He nodded and took a swig of his beer. "That I am."

Mason nodded slowly. "Bet Ashley was relieved."

"You think being married to me would be so bad?" Levi felt something inside him snap as Mason managed to sum up everything that sucked about the situation. Why would Ashley want to be married to him? What made him think he'd be a good husband and partner?

Mason threw up a hand. "Your wedding started as a joke."

So his teammate agreed with him. Nice to know. "Which means it had to end that way too?"

"I just meant that the two of you hadn't so much as dated before you were waving that piece of paper in front of her face, telling her you were married. She's pretty career focused, and the two of you never seemed to hit it off."

Well, except when they were exploring each other's tonsils. She'd liked him just fine then. "When did you turn into Dear Abby?"

Mason grinned. "I have sisters. They have magazines. A guy's got to read something in the john."

The mental image of Mason flipping through a *Cosmo* while in the john was all kinds of wrong. "Way too much information."

They were silent for a minute, watching the action on the casino floor. A bridal party picked their way through the slot machines, all grins and white tulle. Levi hadn't realized until he'd come down here that casinos churned out almost as many brides as they did cocktails. Getting married on the beach was better— and a whole lot quieter.

"I asked her to marry me," he blurted out. "She turned me down."

"Maddie asked me." A big grin split Mason's face. "*I* turned *her* down. When I came to my senses, I went after her and begged her to say *yes*. Sometimes you just have to keep trying."

Since Mason was getting married in two weeks, Maddie's answer was obvious. Too bad going after Ashley wouldn't fix this or get her back. He needed a better plan than just asking her.

"I'm gonna try my luck," he said to Mason and

headed for the slots. Not taking the hint, Mason followed and parked himself on the stool next to Levi's. To stave off more conversation, he fed ten dollars into the machine and punched the buttons. The machine had some kind of star-spangled banner theme, and he half expected fireworks or a marching band to come popping out, but instead he got a row of red, white and blue stars. He was still thinking about that later when he hit. The lights flashed, the sirens whooped, and pretty much every eye in the place turned his way.

"Lucky," Mason drawled.

Levi sure didn't feel lucky. Winning a thousand bucks wasn't what he wanted.

The doors to the casino chapel burst open—to what must be bride number seven hundred for the night—and guests spilled out. The bride and groom wore T-shirts—his with a tuxedo front and hers mimicking a white dress, and the bride had a headband sprouting tulle. Their guests surrounded them, laughing and shouting. You had to smile just looking at them, he thought. Based on the discussion of which buffet the group should hit for the post-wedding celebrations, there wasn't a whole lot of money to spare, but they were smiling, and he'd bet they'd still be smiling in forty years.

Not that he was any kind of marital expert, but he was lucky. He stared at the slip of paper in his hand and went over to the teller's cage to cash it in. He should have given Ashley that kind of wedding. She'd have liked the T-shirts, given her appreciation for their his-and-her swimsuits. Instead, they'd had a fake wedding on the beach, and he hadn't even asked her what kind of memories she really wanted. Or said *I love you*.

Because it was the *I love you*s written on the faces

of the newly married couple that promised everything was going to be okay.

Huh.

Mason elbowed him. "You okay?

The only person Levi was discussing love with was Ashley, so he just grunted in reply. If he got on his bike, he could get up to Virginia in seventeen hours. Fourteen or fifteen if he broke a few speed limits and didn't stop to pee. He could go find Ashley and ask her to marry him. Again. In fact, this time he could bring up love and see what she had to say about that.

Mason elbowed him again, a little harder. Fuck. Any harder and Levi would be sporting broken ribs.

"I have to go," he said. "I've got something to do."

"Someone," Mason said with a smirk.

"Maybe I'm just grossed out watching Gray sext with his bride-to-be." He'd accidentally read a line over the man's shoulder, and no. Just no. Gray flipped him the bird, and Levi said his goodbyes.

The newlyweds in the T-shirts were dancing in the buffet line to a sound track only they could hear. He went over and slipped the bride's mother the thousand bucks. He had a feeling the couple could use it, and they deserved more than ten dollar steak for dinner.

He had eleven hundred miles to come up with a plan to win Ashley back.

16

ASHLEY PARKED HER CAR, mentally counting down the seconds until she made it through her front door. Her town house had a postage-stamp front garden that was all over roses and surrounded by a black iron fence full of Gothic curlicues. It was a little over the top, but she liked it.

Her condo was a skinny three stories, and if she forgot to shut her drapes she gave the neighbors a peep show, but it was hers. Her brain promptly inserted Levi into the picture, and she mentally kicked herself. The man lived in foxholes, base camps and air hangars. When he was stateside, he was either deep undercover, or living on base. He wouldn't give a hoot about her... flowers.

Thank God the day was over. She'd testified about the Central American fiesta some of her coworkers had had going on. She'd felt slightly hypocritical at times, calling them on the carpet for exploring their sexual dark sides, but she and Levi hadn't gotten it on on the taxpayer's dime—or the cartel's. Their mistakes were their own, no thanks to anybody else. At least it was over and she could move on to the next challenge. And yet she felt empty. Work wasn't enough anymore. She couldn't stop thinking about Levi, which made her do stupid things like remember how she'd fallen in love with the big jerk. And *why*. The *why* was the kicker that made her regret pushing him away. Maybe they could have made it work for a little longer, maybe she could have kept her SEAL. For another week, another month, another lifetime. *Stop thinking*. She patted her pocket where she kept Stupidity Exhibit A.

Her cat wandered out to say hello as soon as she made it through the front door, proving that at least one someone was glad to see her. He bumped around her ankles as she turned to the security panel to disarm the alarm. She had thirty seconds to punch in her code or she'd be having date night with the security company's team. Except the alarm was already off. A smiley face blinked at her from the panel. Oookay.

Adrenaline rushed through her as she palmed her service piece, and she forced herself to take a deep breath. Think. What were the odds that burglar had bypassed her system and programmed an emoticon? Rather than, say, cleaning her place out or lying in wait to add her to his list of victims? Mentally she ran through the recent news pieces on crimes, but no one had mentioned a serial killer who left a smiley face behind. Her foot nudged something and she looked down. A burglar who left his steel-toes by her front door.

If she was playing things smart, she'd go outside and call the security company from the relative safety of her car. Let them check her place out. Or she could go looking for the boots' owner. Her heartrate kicked up a notch.

The Siamese meeped at her and bumped her calf again. The cat didn't sense a threat. Or—she eyed the plate by the door—he'd been bribed with tuna fish. She and her burglar were going to have words about the proper care and feeding of cats, because the boots were familiar. Probably. They were standard military issue. That was true. It was possible a random SEAL had broken into her house. And left a message on her alarm panel after feeding her cat.

Unlikely.

There was more evidence in her living room, two socks and a belt laid out to form an arrow pointing up the stairs. Okay. So probably not a burglar. She hid her grin. Encouraging Levi was trouble, but she couldn't stop the feeling of giddy excitement from sweeping through her. He'd come back, and when she found him, she'd know why.

His BDUs waited neatly folded at the top of the stairs. She had no idea why he'd bothered being tidy. Or why she was picking the stuff up. But she was, and she added his T-shirt, then moved down the hall toward her bedroom following the trail of clothing, and…hello. She had herself a pair of navy-blue boxers. With a ring box on top of them. There was a smiley-face Post-it note and a small key stuck to the top of the box. *Don't read anything into it.*

She and her SEAL needed to have words, starting with a lesson on how to knock on the front door. Or call, email or text. The bedroom door was open and she'd bet he'd made himself at home. Honestly, she didn't know whether she should read him the riot act or smother him with kisses. What kind of man committed a felony to get her attention?

Your man, her heart whispered. *He could be* your *man.*

Tamping the hope down, she stepped inside the bedroom. "I could have called the security company to check out my burglar."

And they'd have either thanked her for the view or charged extra depending on which way they swung. She blinked. Levi was naked. She'd kind of figured he had to be since she was holding his clothes in her arms, but…he was *naked.* And sprawled on her bed. With both wrists handcuffed to said bed. Now she knew what the key was for. A grin split his face as he took her in, like he was genuinely happy to see her. Or maybe that smile was because she'd brought his clothes and was carrying a gun. Darn it. She set the stuff down on the dresser.

"Thanks for not shooting me," he drawled. How did he manage to just lie there like it was no big deal? Of course, if she looked like Levi, maybe she'd be happy to let her stuff hang out all over the place too. Good lord, he was spectacular.

"When I said marriage was a pile of laundry, you didn't have to take me literally." What was he doing here and why was she letting him get her hopes up? She should be practical about this. She'd had a long day. Her feet were killing her, her bra strap was attempting to carve a second Grand Canyon into her rib cage, and she was three pounds too heavy for her skirt, which made her painfully aware of the waistband. She'd been looking forward to losing her own clothes and dating her tub. Instead, she got Levi—and that was just another word for heartbreak.

He shrugged, and the handcuffs clinked. She couldn't help but notice that these ones weren't purple. "I didn't want to scare you."

"So losing your clothes in my living room was a public service?" Whatever his reasons for being here, they clearly didn't include turning over a new leaf.

He winked at her. "Absolutely."

The man was incorrigible. It would serve him right if she left him tied up. Instead of leaving, however, she strolled closer. Levi naked was always worth looking at and he made her pulse race. She flicked a cuff. "I see you've rethought your position on kink."

"I brought presents," he coaxed.

"Your dirty laundry?" She was *not* going to ask about the ring. It was childish, and she knew it, but Levi could drive her crazy in under thirty seconds and that was a gift right there.

He nodded toward her desk, the one that sat right in front of the window. The *open* window. Her next-door neighbor had a perfect view of naked Levi if the woman happened to look out.

"I like my place," she snapped, striding over to the window and closing the blinds. Sharing was *not* in her vocabulary, not tonight, not if there was any chance Levi might be here because he'd realized he was *hers*.

"It's great," he said agreeably.

"And I don't want to have to move." She rattled the blinds to make her point. "Close. The. Curtains."

He just grinned at her. "We had sex on a beach, Dixie. It's a little late to be shy now."

"*I* had an orgasm on the beach. There was no naked penis involved." Wait. That hadn't come out right.

"I'm mixing things up." He spread his arms as wide as the cuffs would allow. She probably needed to get a bigger bed. Or a smaller SEAL. "And I'll give you another orgasm. Three, if you ask me nicely."

"I'm not in the mood to ask you for anything," she informed him, inspecting the display on her desk. He'd brought a red plastic sand pail filled with ice and a bottle of very nice champagne. The dozen red roses matched the bucket, although his flower-arranging skills sucked. He'd lined the twelve flowers up in a row.

"You missed a bow on your penis."

He looked down. "Would that have helped? Because I'm willing to take suggestions."

She was tired, she was stressed, and he made her feel hopeful. Damn it.

"What are you doing here?"

"I'M NAKED." IF SHE hadn't noticed that, they had bigger problems. Okay. *He* had bigger problems. He honestly hadn't considered the open curtains when he'd cuffed himself to Ashley's bed, but was it really a big deal if her neighbor saw?

"You sure are." She popped the champagne open in one smooth, practiced move. She didn't sound impressed—or look at him. This mission was not going to plan.

"You could get naked, too. That's what married people do. Although you could keep the shoes." Because he really, really liked those shoes. The heels were four inches of come-fuck-me-pretty-please goodness and the leather might be boring beige but some very sexy straps crisscrossed her instep and wrapped around her ankle. When she'd reached over, he'd spotted little zippers running up her heels. Tugging those zippers down with his teeth had suddenly shot to the top of his fantasy list.

She sat down on the bed, still holding the bottle. The *bottom* of the bed and a good four feet away from him. On the plus side, she was wearing another one of those suits he liked so much. The skirt hugged her ass and her thighs, stopping just below her knees, and the jacket was buttoned tightly over her breasts. He wasn't sure what she was wearing underneath it, but he'd really like to find out.

"We're not married," she said.

They could fix that. "I'd like to be."

"Uh-huh." She lifted the bottle to her mouth and stared at him over the rim. "I put you on my to-do list." He had no idea what that meant, but apparently it was her cue to drink, because she took a swig of the champagne. "We need to be clear on a few things."

"Shoot," he said, which probably wasn't his smartest comment. Ashley was more than capable of shooting him if she felt like it. He'd spent his first twenty minutes in her condo unloading the various weapons she had stashed around the place. He was all for home security, but he didn't need her plugging him if she misinterpreted his small rewiring of her home security system.

"One. I can handle my life myself." She took another swig from the bottle and paused. "My skirt is killing me. I had to get all dressed up for the hearing today."

"Take it off," he suggested. It wasn't like she didn't know he was thinking it. For Christ's sake, he was naked. He had no secrets. She shot him a look as if he wasn't supposed to say those things, but he'd always been honest with her. She set the bottle on the floor and stood up. It got incrementally harder to breath when her fingers went to the buttons on the front of her jacket and slipped the first one free. She hesitated, but her having second thoughts wasn't part of his plan.

"Got it," he said gruffly, to distract her. "You can

take care of business on your own, but feel free to pass the crap stuff to me."

"You're going to do the mental equivalent of taking out the trash for me?" The second button popped free.

"If that's what you need," he agreed. She was too far away. He jerked his chin toward the bed beside him. "Come up here."

She ignored him and shrugged out of her jacket. She had one of those silky little shells underneath, the kind of shirt that looked more like underwear than anything. The suit jacket might be practical navy blue, but her shirt was red. Made him wonder what color her bra was.

"Two, I don't need a hero." She stalked closer when she said this, hands on her hips.

"Roger that, but I could damn sure use a heroine like you, if you'll give me another chance. You got the key handy?"

She sighed and patted her chest. "Tucked it in my bra, sailor."

"You want to uncuff me? Or come over here and ride me?"

She grinned. "Maybe I'm saving you for Christmas."

The holiday was months away. "I sure hope you're the kind of gal who peeks at her presents."

She made a face, but she came up to the top of the bed and turned around, presenting him with her backside. "Unzip," she commanded.

"Houston, we have a problem," he said dryly, rattling his cuffs.

She shot him a look over her shoulder. "Use your imagination."

"We need a new dare," he said roughly, leaning forward and grabbing the zipper with his teeth. *Challenge accepted*. One swift tug and her skirt hung loose around her hips. She stepped away and let it fall to the ground with a little shimmy that made him curse his stupid handcuff idea. He'd been trying to make a point about being willing to stick, but now her sweet curves were calling his name and it would take him at least thirty seconds to get the cuffs off without her help.

She stepped out of the skirt, bent over and picked it up. She had an amazing ass—and a killer red thong. He groaned. When she whisked her shirt over her head, he was a goner. Her red satin bra matched her panties. He didn't see the key, though, and that was a problem.

"If I beg, will you use the key?"

She smiled. Slowly. His Dixie knew exactly what she was doing to him. "If you want to explore your kinky side, all you have to do is ask."

"Let's play a game." He wiggled his hips. "You bring the champagne and sit here."

Her eyes narrowed. "Is this where I get to interrogate you about why you committed at least one felony and broke into my house?"

"Sure."

She hesitated, but then she climbed up onto the bed and threw a leg over him. The cuffs wouldn't allow him to pull her higher, but that didn't mean he was without options. He curled his lower body up, bumping her into place. She shrieked and champagne splashed on him. "You're gonna need to clean that up."

She wriggled, making herself comfortable and him uncomfortable. "Seriously? No. Don't answer that. Just tell me the rules of the game."

"The name of the game is Never Have I Ever." She squirmed and he groaned. This had better be the world's fastest game or he wasn't going to last. "It's simple. I say something I haven't done. If you've done it, you drink."

Frowning, she eyed the level in the champagne bottle. "You should have bought a bigger bottle."

"I bought you the good stuff, too. Now shut up and listen, because I'm going first."

She opened her mouth to protest, but he wasn't kidding. He had something to say and she was going to listen. Bringing his knees up, he nudged her. Just a little. She landed off balance on his chest, mouth inches from his. Before she could catch her breath, he started.

"Never have I ever… I've never fallen in love before."

She frowned, lifted the bottle to her mouth, and paused. "I'm not sure my grammar's good enough for this."

"You been in love before?"

She shoved upright and jammed a finger into his chest. "Who's interrogating who here? And what does *before* mean? Before what?"

Maybe this would have been easier if he'd waited until she finished the bottle. "Just drink. You're spoiling my plan."

She hesitated—the woman had serious control issues—but then she drank.

"Never have I ever…asked the woman I love to marry me."

She drank. "I can safely say I've never proposed to a woman."

"Never have I ever not fallen for you."

She got that cute little wrinkle between her eyebrows again. Then she scooted around on his lap again. "Your grammar's killing me. I think I need a diagram."

"I'm trying to be romantic," he gritted out, because

the way she was sliding her red thong—and other things—over his dick had cut off the supply of blood to his brain.

"Huh." The frown got deeper. "Roses and champagne are a little clichéd, don't you think? Plus I'm not sure felony burglary really endears you to me. What if I hadn't figured out it was you?"

"You didn't answer the last question," he pointed out. "You have to confess—or drink. Do you love me? I gotta be perfectly honest about one thing, babe."

She glared at him. Shit. Was she teary-eyed? "If you change your mind after saying all that stuff, I will kill you."

He shook his head. "Not a chance. I love you. I think I've been in love with you since you kissed the hell out of me in that alley behind the Best Ride. I know you weren't planning on getting married on Fantasy Island, and neither was I, but it turned out to be the best damned accident of my life, and I'd like to do it again. On purpose. If you could take a chance on me? I'd be grateful."

ASHLEY TRIED TO focus on Levi, trying to read his expression. "You don't do relationships."

"You're gonna be my first. And my last." A smile tugged at the corner of his mouth.

"You're serious?" *Please, please be serious.*

"Babe, that's what the handcuffs are all about." She must have looked blank, because he continued. "I'm here to stay. I'm sticking for as long as you want me."

Oh. God. If she cried, she'd have to kill herself.

He wasn't done talking, though. "When we were on

the island, *you* said the only way I'd stick was if I was handcuffed."

"So you thought you'd prove your undying love for me by handcuffing yourself to my bed?"

"Something like that." He grinned, looking more than a little sheepish.

This was probably the point where she should trot out an *I love you* speech of her own. Because she did. Love him. But she didn't have any cute games or clever words. All she had were her feelings for him.

"You gonna say something?" he asked when she just sat there and stared at him.

"You really want to get married?" Because it was impulsive and reckless and…she wanted to do it. She really did. She just needed the right reason.

"I love you. I just drove fifteen hours straight to get here so I could tell you."

"Do I have to give you a speech?"

"Nope. All you have to do is tell me that you love me back."

She swung off him and padded toward her abandoned jacket. "You're headed the wrong way," he said. "In case you didn't realize it."

There was a note of vulnerability in his voice she hadn't heard before, so she made her errand quick. The little box was right where she'd left it, tucked in the pocket of her jacket. Maybe this was stupid. On the other hand, he'd handcuffed himself to the bed and she definitely wanted to take the chance he was offering. Take a chance on them, take a chance on love.

"I love you," she admitted softly, returning to the bed. "I have something to show you."

Flipping the box open, she turned it around so he

could see the ring. When she'd seen it, it had made her think of Levi and their time on the island. The band was silver, but she'd fallen in love with the green emerald in the middle. It was the color of palm trees, and it made her think of the island. Of him.

Shoot. Maybe she shouldn't have done it. "I know it's silly."

He looked up at her. "It's perfect. Are you asking me to marry you, Dixie?"

"Yes." She sucked in a deep, tremulous breath. "I am."

He groaned. "You couldn't have told me this *before* I went to all this trouble and tied myself to the bed?"

"You're a US Navy SEAL. I'll bet you can get out of those cuffs in under thirty seconds. *Before* I lose my bra and panties."

"You're on." He grinned at her. "What do I get when I win?"

"Me," she whispered, and it didn't take him thirty seconds. More like two, so the man had definitely cheated. She shrieked when his arms came around her, and God, she hoped her neighbors had remembered to close their windows.

"You really gonna put a ring on me?" he growled, pulling her back against him and threading his fingers through hers.

"You bet." The air left her lungs, something happier and headier replacing it. Love. Affection. Tenderness. And a sense of homecoming that had nothing to do with where she was, and everything to do with the man holding her. She slid the ring onto his finger, admiring the fit.

"Just so you know," he said, and she knew a promise when she heard one, "I always collect on my bets."

"You've got me." Screw it. She wasn't a girly girl and she was more than a little impatient, so she put his ring on her finger. The pink pearl in its circle of diamonds winked up at her, and she smiled.

"Each other," he allowed, brushing a kiss over her mouth.

"Yes," she said immediately, wrapping her arms around him because holding on to him was the best chance, the best dare she'd ever made. "Win or lose, we'll always have each other."

* * * * *

#895 COWBOY ALL NIGHT
Thunder Mountain Brotherhood
by Vicki Lewis Thompson
When Aria Danes hires a legendary horse trainer to work with her new foal, she isn't expecting sexy, easygoing Brant Ellison. But when they're together, it's too hot for either to maintain their cool!

#896 A SEAL'S DESIRE
Uniformly Hot!
by Tawny Weber
Petty Officer Christian "Cowboy" Laramie is the hero Sammie Jo Wilson always looked up to. When she needs his help, she finds out she is the only woman Laramie thinks is off-limits...but for how long?

#897 TURNING UP THE HEAT
Friends With Benefits
by Tanya Michaels
Pastry chef Phoebe Mars and sophisticated charmer Heath Jensen are only pretending to date in order to make Phoebe's ex jealous. But there's nothing pretend about the sexy heat between them!

#898 IN THE BOSS'S BED
by J. Margot Critch
Separating business and pleasure proves to be impossible for Maya Connor and Jamie Sellers. When they can't keep their passion out of the boardroom, scandal threatens to destroy everything they've worked for.

REQUEST YOUR FREE BOOKS!
2 FREE NOVELS PLUS 2 FREE GIFTS!

HARLEQUIN®

Blaze

red-hot reads!

YES! Please send me 2 FREE Harlequin® Blaze® novels and my 2 FREE gifts (gifts are worth about $10). After receiving them, if I don't wish to receive any more books, I can return the shipping statement marked "cancel." If I don't cancel, I will receive 4 brand-new novels every month and be billed just $4.74 per book in the U.S. or $5.21 per book in Canada. That's a savings of at least 14% off the cover price. It's quite a bargain. Shipping and handling is just 50¢ per book in the U.S. and 75¢ per book in Canada.* I understand that accepting the 2 free books and gifts places me under no obligation to buy anything. I can always return a shipment and cancel at any time. Even if I never buy another book, the two free books and gifts are mine to keep forever.

150/350 HDN GH2D

Name	(PLEASE PRINT)	
Address		Apt. #
City	State/Prov.	Zip/Postal Code

Signature (if under 18, a parent or guardian must sign)

Mail to the **Reader Service:**
IN U.S.A.: P.O. Box 1867, Buffalo, NY 14240-1867
IN CANADA: P.O. Box 609, Fort Erie, Ontario L2A 5X3

Want to try two free books from another line?
Call 1-800-873-8635 or visit www.ReaderService.com.

* Terms and prices subject to change without notice. Prices do not include applicable taxes. Sales tax applicable in N.Y. Canadian residents will be charged applicable taxes. Offer not valid in Quebec. This offer is limited to one order per household. Not valid for current subscribers to Harlequin Blaze books. All orders subject to credit approval. Credit or debit balances in a customer's account(s) may be offset by any other outstanding balance owed by or to the customer. Please allow 4 to 6 weeks for delivery. Offer available while quantities last.

Your Privacy—The Reader Service is committed to protecting your privacy. Our Privacy Policy is available online at www.ReaderService.com or upon request from the Reader Service.

We make a portion of our mailing list available to reputable third parties that offer products we believe may interest you. If you prefer that we not exchange your name with third parties, or if you wish to clarify or modify your communication preferences, please visit us at www.ReaderService.com/consumerchoice or write to us at Reader Service Preference Service, P.O. Box 9062, Buffalo, NY 14240-9062. Include your complete name and address.

He longed to reach for her, but instead he leaned into the van and snagged her hat. "You'll need this."

"Thanks." She settled the hat on her head—instant sexy cowgirl. "Let's go."

Somehow he managed to stop looking at her long enough to put his feet in motion. No doubt about it, he was hooked on her, and they'd only met yesterday.

If she was aware of his infatuation, she didn't let on as they walked into the barn. "I'm excited that we'll be taking him out today. I thought he might have to stay inside a little longer."

"Only if the weather had been nasty. But it's gorgeous." Like *you*. He'd almost said that out loud. Talk about cheesy compliments. "Cade and I already turned the other horses out into the far pasture, but we kept these two in the barn. We figured you should be here for Linus's big moment."

"Thank goodness you waited for me. I would have been crushed if I'd missed this."

"I wouldn't have let that happen." Okay, he was grandstanding a little, but it was true. Nobody at the ranch would have allowed Aria to miss watching Linus experience his first time outside.

"How about Rosie and Herb? Will they come watch?"

"You couldn't keep them away. A foal's first day in the pasture is special. Lexi and Cade are up at the house having breakfast with them, so they'll all come down in a bit." And he'd text them so they'd know she was here.

But not yet. He didn't foresee a lot of opportunities to be alone with her unless he created them. He wanted to savor this moment for a little while longer.

"Brant, can I ask a favor?" She paused and turned to him.

"Sure." He stopped walking.

Taking off her hat, she stepped toward him. "Would you please kiss me?"

With a groan he swept her up into his arms so fast she squeaked in surprise and his hat fell off...again. His mouth found hers and he thrust his tongue deep. His hands slid around her and when he lifted her up, she gave a little hop and wrapped her legs around his hips. Dear God, it felt good to wedge himself between her thighs.

Don't miss COWBOY ALL NIGHT
by New York Times *bestselling author*
Vicki Lewis Thompson, available June 2016 wherever
Harlequin® Blaze® books and ebooks are sold.

www.Harlequin.com

HBEXP0516

Whatever You're Into… Passionate Reads

Looking for more passionate reads from Harlequin®?
Fear not! Harlequin® Presents, Harlequin® Desire and
Harlequin® Blaze offer you irresistible romance stories
featuring powerful heroes.

HARLEQUIN *Presents*.

Do you want alpha males, decadent glamour and jet-set
lifestyles? Step into the sensational, sophisticated world of
Harlequin® Presents, where sinfully tempting heroes ignite a
fierce and wickedly irresistible passion!

HARLEQUIN *Desire*

Harlequin® Desire novels are powerful, passionate and
provocative contemporary romances set against a backdrop of
wealth, privilege and sweeping family saga. Alpha heroes with
a soft side meet strong-willed but vulnerable heroines amid a
dramatic world of divided loyalties, high-stakes conflict and
intense emotion.

HARLEQUIN *Blaze*

Harlequin® Blaze stories sizzle with strong heroines and
irresistible heroes playing the game of modern love and lust.
They're fun, sexy and always steamy.

Be sure to check out our full selection of books
within each series every month!

www.Harlequin.com

HPASSION2016

Reading Has Its Rewards

Earn **FREE BOOKS!**

Register at **Harlequin My Rewards** and submit your Harlequin purchases from wherever you shop to earn points for free books and other exclusive rewards.

Plus submit your purchases from now till May 30th for a chance to win a $500 Visa Card*.

Visit **HarlequinMyRewards.com** today

MYR16R1

Love the Harlequin book
you just read?

Your opinion matters.

Review this book on your favorite
book site, review site, blog or your own
social media properties and share
your opinion with other readers!